# Dark Lies

CLARISSA WILD

Copyright © 2021 Clarissa Wild
All rights reserved.
ISBN: 9798717250177

This is a work of fiction. Names, characters, places and incidents are either the product of the author's imagination or are used fictitiously. Any resemblance to actual events, places, organizations, or person, whether living or dead, is entirely coincidental.

All rights reserved. No part of this book may be reproduced, transmitted in any form or by any means, electronic or mechanical, including photocopying, recording, or by any information storage retrieval system. Doing so would break licensing and copyright laws.

# PLAYLIST

"Pressure" by MISSIO
"Nature" by MISSIO
"Letting Go" by MISSIO
"In The Woods Somewhere" by Hozier
"Dangerous Game" by Klergy
"Light Of The Seven" by Ramin Djawadi
"Main Theme – Westworld" by Ramin Djawadi
"The Fault Line" by The Rigs
"Bury" by Unions
"Burning Desire" Lana Del Rey
"Video Games" by Lana Del Rey
"Pneumothorax" by Blueneck
"Bloc Party" by The Pioneers (M83 Remix)
"The Labyrinth Song" by Asaf Avidan
"Something In The Way (Epic Trailer Version)" by Samuel Kim Music
"Familiar" by Agnes Obel

# ONE

## Amelia

My body shakes vigorously, and I'm unable to contain the dread building inside.

"You were in my home?" I ask. "When?"

"Enough questions. Ask them later." He presses a kiss to my shoulder and then throws the blanket off him. "I'm going to take a shower. Get some sleep."

He slides off the bed while I clutch the blanket close, afraid of what'll happen if I let go. If I let my mind allow these thoughts to invade.

Because deep down inside, I know he's a bad guy.

A guy who seems capable of doing anything to get his way.

Even if it means setting someone up to become a killer.

A chill runs up and down my spine, and as the door to the bathroom closes and the shower is turned on, I throw the blanket off me and jump out of bed. I can't stay here. No matter how desperately he wants me to or how good I felt when I kissed him, I have to escape.

So I search his room, ripping open everything I find—desk drawers, wardrobes, cabinets. I leave nothing unturned until I find what I'm looking for in the pocket of the pants he just took off: a key.

And not just any key. The key he's carried with him since he first trapped me here in this house. The key that opens all the other rooms where the captives are kept.

I swallow hard, thinking about Anna and what it did to her when I took her with me.

I won't make that same mistake again.

If I ever want to make it out alive, if I want them to be safe, I have to find another way to help them ... from the outside.

I get up from the floor and grab my dress to put it on again, but this time, I don't make the same mistake as last time. Instead of putting on my high heels, I grab a bunch of socks from his wardrobe, layer them over my feet, and slide on a pair of his training sneakers.

And without any further thoughts, I run.

\*\*\*

# Eli

Stripping off my shirt and jacket, I throw them in the corner of the bathroom and stare in the mirror at the man I've become for a moment. At the man who moved mountains to get a girl to confess ... but at what price?

I turn around and look at the scars that cover my skin. Some old ... some fresh. Every muscle that flexes sends a blazing trail of pain down my back, and I make a face at the thought of doing it all over again.

A necessary evil for a necessary crime.

Even the punisher must be punished for his sins.

I sigh to myself and close my eyes, preparing for what comes after I'm finished. And I turn on the shower and step under it.

The water rushes over my naked body, covering me in a sheen of warmth. For the first time in a long time, I don't feel overwhelmed by the pain. Instead, I'm reminded of the warmth I felt when she was on my lap, of how amazing it felt to bury myself inside her ... of how much I really wanted to wrap my arms around her and never let go.

When I brought her here, I thought I could do this—that I could fuck her and use her and make her confess with ease. But she was more challenging than I imagined, and it took more than just my body to make her yield.

Groaning, I stare down at the water pooling at my feet, wondering how I got here. Why I ever made the decision to make her fall, bring her in, and break her. If it was all worth it.

Because I haven't just added scars on top of scars to my back.

I've added scars to my heart.

The moment she kissed me, I lost the battle, the will to resist, and I let her. In fact, I loved it so much that I came back for seconds, for thirds ... I needed more and more. I still do. The more I take, the more I want, and the more she's willing to give, which leads to this vicious cycle neither of us can escape.

And when I go out there, I know I will need to make a decision about what to do with her. Decide whether I'm going to set her free or keep her for my own selfish needs.

But would she ever want me the way I want her?

Could she ever love the man beneath the beast?

The man who made her confess?

I run my hand over my face and rinse off, determined not to dwell on it further. The fact is, I've already made my decision. Even if I tell myself I still have time, I don't.

Because I already knew long ago what I was going to do ... And that it wasn't going to be her choice, but mine. I don't easily give up something that's supposed to be mine to keep.

Maybe that makes me a monster, but I don't care. I know what I want, and I'm willing to hurt for it, die for it ... kill for it.

I've already stepped over the line, so why would it

matter if I keep doing it?

But a little voice inside my head whispers at me in the dark.

*Don't do it. You'll regret it.*
*Not for you. You know exactly what you want.*
*But you'll regret it … for her.*

I frown and glare at the wall in front of me.

Since when do I have a conscience?

I don't, and no amount of thinking will change that fact.

So I grunt as I turn off the shower, then grab a towel to head back into my bedroom and find sweet relief in her embrace. But the moment I open the door, I'm surprised to find an empty bed.

Open wardrobes.

Clothes scattered all around.

A wide-open door.

Just like my mouth.

\*\*\*

## Amelia

Through the dark night, I run past the bushes and along the trees, back through the same forest I traversed last time. But this time, I came prepared. I snuck out through the garage after stealing a map from one of the cabinets there. I know exactly where to go now. Not too far away from where I got last time. But now, no guard is on my tail. No one to call me in or chase me down to the beach and catch me just before I make it off.

The guards were having lunch in the kitchen when I escaped, and Eli won't even notice I'm gone until it's too late.

With a bolstered heart, I storm through the woods without looking back. Even though every step hurts because of what I'm leaving behind, I don't dare say that out loud, to ever utter the words "I deserved to be here."

I can't. Not until I know the truth.

And for that, I need to go back to the place where it all began. Home.

So I run and run until my breath falters, my legs almost buckle underneath me, and my heart almost beats out of my chest. Even if my body is at its end, I refuse to quit because I know there is a way out. There has to be.

Suddenly, I spot it. The small pier I've been looking for, the one on the map.

It isn't much, just a few wood planks stuck into the water, but there's a boat attached to a rope. And I'm going to steal it.

***

# Eli

I sprint through the woods as fast as I can with the guards on my tail. I didn't tell anyone what happened because there was no time. I had to catch up with her, no matter the cost. I knew where she was headed and what she was about to do.

She was going back there, back to where I caught her, but this time, she'd find an exit. The only one I'd left behind in case I'd ever need one. Never has regret been this strong.

Adrenaline pumps through my veins as I try to get there on time. I ran outside in a mere shirt, a pair of boxers, and some loafers. That's how quick I was to chase her.

And it still isn't fast enough.

Because the moment I spot her, she's already halfway on her way across the water in my fucking boat. All by herself, with no one and nothing to help her if she fails to get across.

"Amelia!" I yell as I stand on the beach and watch her turn around.

The look on her face is precious, scornful, yet full of sorrow.

As though it pains her as much to do this.

As though this is a final goodbye.

But if there's one thing she clearly doesn't understand about me, it's that I will never stop hunting her. Not now. Not ever.

# TWO

*Amelia*

The water sloshes around, causing the boat to sway heavily from side to side, and I have trouble holding the railing. The moon is my only light to guide my way across this water. I don't know where I am or where I'm going, but the way forward is the only way I can take.

Even if I'm alone and scared to death.

I don't want to think about what happens if I don't find land soon because this boat carries very few supplies. When I checked the storage, I found a few cans of soup, but that's it. No phone or anything to contact anyone with, unfortunately. The rest were all supplies for the boat, a simple emergency kit, and a blanket from a waterproof container to keep me warm.

But there is no time to try to get warm in the cold draft rushing over the water because I need to steer the boat in the right direction too often. Strong winds force the boat to turn, sometimes almost capsizing it, and I need all my weight to keep it on track. I'm not trained in boating, so this storm is more frightening than anything I've faced.

A large wave crashes against the side, and it whips the boat up so far that I lose my foothold. I slip on the deck, and I'm thrown off as the water whisks me away. The cold water envelops my body and enters my lungs before I know what's happening. But I refuse to let go without a fight.

I push to the surface, gasping for air. Coughing out loud, I take a few breaths and try to orient myself. The waves crashing into me pull me farther and farther away from the boat. Yet it's still within my reach if I can just muster up that last bit of energy and use it for swimming back.

Adrenaline pumps through my veins as I force myself to swim toward it, throwing all my weight and strength into each stroke. Every breath I take feels harder as the cold water weighs down on me and makes my muscles contract.

Finally, I manage to grab the tiny ladder on the side of the boat and pull myself up using sheer determination. I grasp the railing and pull myself on board again.

I cough and heave as the water leaves my throat. My body slumps into a pile of cold mush on the deck while the boat swishes against the rugged waters, the wind mercilessly frigid and deadly.

And for a few seconds, I almost wish I had never decided to take this boat and flee. Then I would still be in the comfort of that luxurious house with a warm blanket tucked around me and as much food as I could eat.

I'm too scared to admit that I miss it, even if only a little.

Because I would still be very much alive there.

And right now—on this boat—I'm not so sure I'm going to survive.

But I'm alive for now, staring up at the night's sky breaking open with rain as I lie here on this deck. And I will not go out until I've taken my very last fighting breath.

Because that's who I am. A warrior. A survivor.

\*\*\*

# Eli

"How long is this going to take?" I bark at one of my guards as he casually stuffs his backpack with supplies.

He throws me a look, then continues packing as if there's no rush.

"C'mon," I growl. "The longer she's out there, the more chance there is of her getting away."

"I am well aware, sir," the guard replies. "We're going in for the pursuit."

"What are you waiting for then?" I yell, pointing at the

door. "She's already out there on the water with nothing but a silly boat. I need her safe and sound."

"Sir, please calm down," he says.

The calm in his voice only lights the fire blazing inside my heart. "Calm down? I will not calm the fuck down while she is out there, all by herself, during a raging storm! She could die!"

"They know, all right?" Tobias interjects. "And they know what they're doing."

His warm hand rests unwelcome on my tense shoulder.

I jerk free from his grip. "Yes, I'm quite aware of my own employees' qualifications, thank you."

"You hired them specifically for this purpose," he says, cocking his head. "So let them do it."

"If they'd done their job, she wouldn't have escaped in the first place," I spit back, eyeing the guard from the sidelines while he puts his backpack on and tells everyone to round up.

"She escaped with a key, no?" Tobias raises his brow as he taps me on the chest. "That means *you* should have been more careful."

I swat his finger away. "I don't need you lecturing me. I know I misjudged her."

"She did what anyone would do in her position. A caged animal will always try to get out."

"She's not an animal," I say through gritted teeth. I'm tempted to throw a right hook at him, but when my hands clench to fists, all the guards in the hallway look at me like they're waiting for me to act. Like everyone here is waiting for me to lose my mind. And I refuse to go there.

I shake my head at him. "Never mind."

I march off before I start throwing punches. I'm that pissed off. Not just at Tobias and the guards but also at myself for believing I could trust her for one second.

How could I just leave that key in my pocket?

Why didn't I bring it with me into the shower?

Was I that forgetful? Or did I make a conscious choice because I wanted to see what she'd do?

I don't make mistakes, yet I did with her.

As I slam the door to my study shut, I grunt while pacing around, almost tearing my hair out. I wish I knew why I did what I did, but I have no idea. Maybe I was still lost in thought, lost in emotion, lost in … her.

Because when I lay there in bed with her, all I could think about was how badly I wanted to stay there and how much I enjoyed feeling her luscious curves spoon against mine. My cock was already hard and ready to take her again, and again, and again.

I wanted nothing more.

In fact, I still want nothing more than to bury myself inside her until we both scream out each other's names and want nothing more than to fall into each other's arms and stay there for all eternity.

And now she's gone.

Vanished into a midnight storm as if she never even existed in the first place.

Even after she knew what she had done, and I was there to help her pull it out of her, she still chose to run from me. Why?

Why can't I give her what she needs?

Rage overwhelms me, and I pick up the desk and throw it over, howling madly.

My chest is tight, and my heart aches as I tower over the mess I made, wishing I could chase her myself and bring her back where she belongs.

But the helicopter would take hours to get here, and by that time, she'll be long gone.

Either she'll have made it to land, or she'll have been swept away by the sea.

The mere thought of losing her to the water chokes me up, and I grab my throat while closing my eyes, forcing these thoughts to stay at bay.

When did I start to feel so much for this girl? Why did these tears form in my eyes now that I realize I may have lost her forever?

"Fuck!" I yell. Turning toward the fireplace, I grab the nearest glass in my vicinity and chuck it straight at the fire.

I stare at the flames in front of me. They remind me of my soul.

Suddenly, the door creaks. I sigh out loud without looking to see who it is. "What do you want?"

But when a soft voice speaks, I look up. "Sorry, sir, I did not mean to bother you."

"Mary," I say, and I lean back up from the fireplace and

pat down my clothes. "What are you—"

Her eyes travel across the room and scour the mess I made of my own desk, interrupting my thoughts as my cheeks begin to glow.

"Sorry, I …"

"Oh, no need to apologize," she briskly says, forming a gentle smile on her face. "I understand. After what you have been through … anyone would be upset."

I close my eyes and rub my forehead. "Please ignore it. I'll clean it up myself."

"Oh, no, sir. You're far too busy trying to get Amelia back," she says as she bustles inside with a broom. "Besides, I was about to sweep this area anyway. Might as well make it a big cleaning operation." She adds a giggle at the end.

With a long-drawn-out sigh, I nod. I'll allow it for once. Normally, I don't enjoy company, and I only allow the assistants to come inside to clean when I'm away, but I'll make an exception now. Better for her to find this mess than Tobias. He'd give me an earful, one I am not interested in hearing. Though I'm sure he could hear me yell from all the way across the hall. Maybe Mary could too.

As she toils away, I gaze at her work for a moment, wondering how on earth I ever found someone to work so diligently and without much complaint. The others could take a lesson from her.

"I'll give you a raise," I say out of the blue.

She looks up, her pupils dilated as she clutches her chest. "You … catch me off guard, sir. You don't need to do that for me."

"No, but I want to," I reply. "You've been of great help with the girls."

"Thank you," she says as she quickly stands. "Really, thank you so much."

I wave it off. "It's only appropriate. After all the work you've done."

"I do it with pleasure, sir," she replies, smiling.

I raise one brow and lower the other. "With pleasure? You haven't forgotten what we do here, right?"

She nods and clutches her fingers. "Of course not, sir. Tobias made sure I wouldn't forget."

Tobias usually instructs our staff about our plans and business.

"And I pride myself on knowing how this House operates, as it does God's work."

I snort and look away. "God's work ... but one of them is escaping as we speak."

"She'll be back," Mary says.

I cock my head. "How do you know?"

She shrugs. "I just feel it. She's the only one you've had this connection with."

I frown and stare at her for a moment when she suddenly palms her face and covers her mouth. "I should not have said that."

I laugh it off. "It's fine. It'd be hard not to notice with the amount of time I've spent with her."

"I just hope I have not offended you, sir." She brushes

the floor even harder. "I just mean … well, I've seen how she reacts to you, your name. She seems quite infatuated with you."

I sigh out loud and shake my head. "If only that were true."

"Oh, she is," she reiterates, recapturing my attention. "I know what it looks like when a woman is falling for someone. And she was … falling harder than she might have been able to handle. Maybe that's why she felt she needed to escape. After all, what can be scarier than falling for someone you're not supposed to fall for?"

The left side of my lip quirks up into a smile. Maybe she's right.

If so, maybe … just maybe … Amelia will return of her own free will.

And if not, I'm just going to have to drag her back with me.

# THREE

## *Amelia*

When my eyes finally open again, my lungs drag in a large breath. I cough violently, lurching up to expel the water still stuck in my throat. I'm shivering, and my clothes are completely soaked. But the storm has passed, and the sun shines.

Have I been out that long?

I blink a couple of times to get used to the light while taking in my surroundings. I'm still on the boat, so I guess I made it out alive. But it's no longer rhythmically swaying back and forth across the waves. In fact, it's come to a complete standstill.

I rub the salt from my eyes and scramble to my feet. I'm still wobbly from my ordeal, and my muscles ache as I walk to the edge of the banister. But any pain fades compared to the excitement rushing through my veins the second I spot the trees up ahead.

*I made it ashore.*

A broad smile forms on my lips as I peer over the edge at the sandy beach below the boat and then the horizon in front of me, which seems like nothing but forest for miles on end. But it's nothing I haven't faced before, and I know there will be an end. Somewhere inside that forest or beyond is a road, and when I find it, it's going to take me home.

Happiness swells within me as I clutch the banister, almost ready to jump off. But then my brain kicks back into action and reminds me that there's still a difficult journey up ahead. I don't know how long it will be until I find any help, let alone a door to knock on, so I must go prepared.

I rush back into the storage compartment and grab the sturdiest bag I can find to load it with the tin cans and any other supplements on board, including some medicine and a blanket. Unfortunately, I find no spare clothes, so I'll have to do with what I'm wearing now. I'll warm myself up by walking. Maybe I can finally exert the pent-up energy from spending all this time locked in that small room.

With all my supplies in a bag, I hop off the deck and start walking. The pine forest beyond is dark and looks completely unkempt, as though there hasn't been a soul in ages. Sunlight barely penetrates the treetops, and I find myself looking up at the slightest of sounds.

Sweat drops litter my forehead in no time, and my

tongue feels like sandpaper. I haven't had anything to drink for quite some time now, and it's starting to weigh down on me. My muscles are cramping more and more with every passing minute, but I refuse to give up.

I've gotten so far already, I can't give up now.

So I continue my trek. There's only one way to survive this: I need to find fresh water. A small brook or even a tiny pool of water will do. Anything to quench my thirst.

But the longer I search, the more I begin to realize it will take me too long to find anything. I've never done this before. I wasn't in the Scouts, and I didn't take any survival classes. I don't even know what to look for besides running water.

The more steps I take, the more my muscles begin to cramp. My breathing is ragged, and I have a hard time concentrating.

Everything begins to spin as if the world itself is turning into mush, but I know it's my eyes that are at fault. With every passing second, I can feel myself fading. I don't have much time left.

"Help!" I call out with whatever energy I have left.

A sudden stump in my way makes me fall to my knees.

It uses too much energy to get up.

To even crouch.

And I find myself lying between a pile of dirt and leaves, wondering if it was all worth it … if my freedom was worth sacrificing my life for.

The light from the sun is fading quickly, but it isn't the

sun going out; it's me.

"Can someone hear me?" I moan as I roll around on the ground, wishing I'd taken something from the mansion that I could've used for communication, like one of those walkie-talkies.

But I was too stupid and too much in a rush to even contemplate the idea, and now I'm here, lying on the ground without so much as a little bit of energy to keep on moving.

My sight goes blurry, even dark at times, and I feel the need to lay my head down and rest. Just rest and rest and do nothing but rest ... for all eternity perhaps.

But I don't want to die here.

All alone and with no one to watch over me.

"Please," I whisper with whatever breath I have left in me, praying someone may find me as even time itself seems to escape me.

And even though sudden rustles in the leaves behind me should have fired off my muscles and made me run, I lie still and fall into a dreamless slumber.

\*\*\*

When I come to again, it feels as though ages have passed. I blink a couple of times to take in the light. The sun is still there, which means it's not night yet.

I open my eyes fully and take in my environment. Wood everywhere, a window to my left. It's a house of some sort.

Suddenly, two eyes bore into mine.

I panic, and with a gasp, I feel my muscles cramping up again when my urge to flee kicks in.

"Calm down," an old man says as he rubs his beard.

Wide-eyed, I try to push myself up, but I'm so damn tired and can't even manage that.

He holds me down, whispering, "Don't move. You've wasted far too much energy." He grabs a cup from the cabinet beside where I'm lying and offers it to me. "Here. Drink."

When the water touches my lips, I gleefully gulp it down, choking on it halfway through.

"Don't drink too fast," he says with a chuckle.

When I'm done, I say, "Thank you."

"That was a close one, wasn't it?"

I nod and ask with a soft voice, "Can I have more?"

He gets up from his seat. "Of course."

I lean up in the bed, despite the pain in my muscles, and look at my surroundings. I'm in what looks like a tiny cabin with a small kitchen, a couch in front of a fireplace, and a single bed where I'm lying right now. "Where am I?"

"My house," he muses as he walks to his little kitchenette and turns on the tap. "I found you unconscious in the woods."

So I really did pass out.

He brings the same cup refilled with water back and hands it to me. "There you go."

"Thanks." I swallow it down in one go, and he laughs again. "How long were you out there?"

"I don't know. I didn't have a watch," I reply, swallowing when he looks at me as if I'm a lost little lamb.

I don't know if I can trust this guy and tell him the truth.

He walks to the closet and takes out something I can only describe as a granny's old flannel. He brings it back to me and places it on the bed. "Here. Put this on. I'll change the sheets of my bed after."

With a frown, I realize what he means. I was soaking wet, my clothes probably covered in dirt and gunk from the ground, and now this man's bed is soiled. Shame turns my cheeks red. "Ah, I'm so sorry," I mutter, quickly throwing off the blankets to witness the onslaught.

"It's okay." He waves it off. "I was the one who put you there."

"But still," I say, rubbing my lips together. "I'll help clean it."

He shakes his head. "No, it's fine. You need to rest. You look like you've been through enough." His eyes glide up and down my torn and tattered glittery dress. A relic from the past. Nothing more. "Where did you say you were from again?"

I swallow. Hard. "I didn't."

His eyes narrow as the situation grows tense.

"Well, you must have someplace you call home," he says.

I clutch the bed, my breathing still not steady, but I don't know whether it's from passing out with dehydration or my adrenaline rush telling me I should run.

"I do …" I sigh. "And I'm trying to find my way back."

He snorts and walks back to his kitchenette. "Well, that seems to be going right for you."

I don't like his tone. "I know. But I'll get there," I say as I get up from the bed. "Thank you for helping me."

I don't want to get on his bad side, so I pretend to be friendly, even with his comments.

"My pleasure," he replies while grabbing a tiny box from the cupboard. "I'm always happy to help." A set of pills drops onto the counter. He looks at them, and so do I … then our eyes connect.

Sweat drops roll down my back. "Where's the bathroom?" I ask.

He points at a tiny door beside the bed, and I quickly get up and walk toward it, never taking my eyes off him, not even as I lock myself inside with the new flannel. I take a breath and force myself to calm down. I'm here now, so I might as well put on the new clothes. A cold, clammy dress won't help me get through this. Besides, he can't reach me here, so this is a moment of respite I'll gladly enjoy.

He knocks on the door two times.

I pause while undressing.

"You okay in there?"

My heart races in my throat, and I sit down on the toilet before my legs buckle under me again. "Yeah."

I don't want to show any weakness.

"I'll make something to eat," he says, and then he

stomps off again.

I breathe out a sigh of relief. The image of the pills dropping from his cabinet flashes through my mind again. Did he intend to give those to me?

The thought did cross my mind. Then again, not every man is out there to get me. But then why does this all feel so unnerving?

I quickly strip off this wet dress and pat myself down with a small towel I find next to a tiny sink. It's better than nothing, though I won't touch my sensitive parts with that. I'll take a proper shower when I get home.

I put on the flannel dress, which looks awful but is better than nothing, and then leave the bathroom. But I stop in my tracks the moment I spot the man with a cell phone against his ear.

"Yeah?"

My eyes widen, and my lips part.

"Missing?"

I stare at him as tears well up in my eyes, and my heart sinks into my shoes.

*Missing.*

Whoever it is on that phone is talking about me.

Eli knows ... and now this man knows too.

The old man glances at me over his shoulder, confirming my suspicions.

I stop breathing for a moment and contemplate whether to steal the phone and run or stay and pray for mercy.

The man just glares at me as though he's already made

up his mind while my eyes glance back and forth between him and the door, thinking about my options. That man is probably much faster than I am in my current condition. He'd probably catch me before I managed to escape.

Instead, I whisper, shaking my head, "Please ... Please, don't tell him I'm here."

# FOUR

## ELI

"Is Amelia there?" I bark into my phone. I don't even care to ask how he's doing. All I care about is finding her. "She's missing."

"Missing?" the guy replies, clearly unimpressed by my rage.

"Yeah, a petite girl with black hair, rosy cheeks, pink lips. She stole one of our boats and fled the island. She's likely traveling through the woods. Did you see anything?"

I hold my breath while he groans. "No, nothing that I know of."

I sigh out loud.

"I'll keep an eye out for her."

"Call me if you spot her," I reply.

"Of course."

I disconnect the call and stare at the phone for a second,

almost squishing it in my hands until it breaks. I have to remain calm and keep my cool because exploding won't help. She's gone either way.

"Did the guard see her?" Tobias asks, interrupting my train of thought.

"No," I say, and I pass by him.

"Where are you going?" he asks.

"To my study."

He frowns, trying to follow me. "Why?"

"To think." I don't need him to chaperone me.

He grabs my shoulder and stops me in my tracks. "Don't do this."

"Do what?" I bark back.

He raises a brow. "Don't think I don't know what you do there. We all do it in our own way." His fingers squeeze against my shoulder blades, close to where the scars are, and I hiss in pain.

"Then you know why I must," I retort, shaking his fingers off.

"Haven't you punished yourself enough?" he says, raising his brows at me while blocking my way. "Eli … I care about you."

"And I care about *her*," I say, throwing him a look.

He sighs. "I know what it feels like to lose someone you care about."

"Maybe … But I still have a chance to get her back." I gaze at him from underneath my eyelashes. "And every second only makes the chance slimmer and slimmer."

"I know, but the guards are doing everything they can to find her," he reassures me.

"We need more boats. I should be out there looking for her," I growl.

"I know," he says, and he pulls me in for a bro-hug. "It's all coming. Just not as fast as we want."

I push him off me. "I need to do this." I walk farther toward my study.

"Why?" he asks. "Why do you feel so guilty?"

In a fit of rage, I spin on my heels, and yell, "Because I made her remember exactly what she did!"

His eyes widen as he freezes to the floor. "*All* of it?"

I nod.

"How did she react?"

"Not good. Obviously." I close my eyes and take in a deep breath.

"You feel guilty," he says.

I hate that he can read me so well. That he knows exactly what I'm thinking and feeling without the need for me to say even a single word.

Maybe that's why he's always so good with the girls who come to our House. He always gets through to people so easily, unlike me.

I blink a couple of times and turn around again. "Let me know when the helicopter arrives."

Before he can say another word, I escape into my study and close the door. I can't breathe a sigh of relief even though I want to so desperately.

My little angle is out there all by herself, alone, afraid, and struggling to survive. And I can't do anything to help her. She won't let me ... because I'm the one who chased her away.

"Fuck!" I slam the door with a fist and march to the fireplace, stuffing the hot iron inside the flames again.

I know I shouldn't do this, I don't want to do this, but my conscience weighs down on me. And the only way to make the heartache go away ... is with pain.

Suddenly, someone knocks on my door, and I stand again, hiding the iron with my body. I don't need more judgment from Tobias, and I know he's itching to let me know what he thinks.

But I'm surprised when Soren pokes his head inside.

He holds up a key.

I frown. "What's that?" Then it hits me. "The jet ski!"

I forgot we even had one. It's rarely used.

Soren nods, and he clutches the key and points at himself.

"You'll go?" I ask. He's the only one who can operate that thing. I've never managed to get the hang of it because it belonged to him, and I didn't see the need. But I wish I had used it more now. It could mean the difference between finding her alive ... or dead.

Soren's face turns serious, and he nods again.

He's doing this for me. To save Amelia and bring her back.

I march over to him. "The water current should've led

her straight to the guard east of our island," I say. "He says she's not there, but I don't trust him. You have to go check."

He grunts in agreement.

"Bring her back," I say as I squeeze his shoulder tight. "I know you can do it."

He gives me an even firmer nod, and I know then and there that he will do his utmost best to get her back safely into my arms.

\*\*\*

## Amelia

The man puts his phone in his pocket while I shiver in place, frozen to the floor.

"T-Thank you," I mutter, hoping he won't turn around and call them in the end.

He pauses and briefly gazes at me before continuing to gather some supplies from a big box near the door. Then he rips a shotgun off the wall. My eyes widen. I grab ahold of the kitchen counter, my eyes darting around the room, searching for a weapon or a way out as I face death in the eyes.

But then the door opens, and the man steps outside.

"I'll be back in a few," he growls, and he slams the door shut behind him, leaving me in complete disarray.

*Where is he going?*

*What is going on?*

No time to waste on thoughts. He could come back at any moment.

I start rummaging through all of his things to find a clue as to who he really is and where I am. Maybe he has some documents somewhere that could prove if he's just a guy or one of Eli's guards.

Because that was definitely him on the phone … and that was no random phone call.

Eli is searching for me, which means I have no time to waste.

I go through his closets, under the bed, and every drawer—nothing is left unturned. I find a loaf of bread and some cheese in one of the cupboards and cut some up on a clean plate. I chow it down as quickly as possible and follow it up with a large cup of water. I checked the fridge, but I don't know if I can trust what's in there. I stuff everything that's safe into a bag I found underneath the bed. I don't want to steal from this man, but I need to get out as soon as possible before Eli's guards find me here and take me back to him.

So I grab a coat hanging on a hook and put it on along with a pair of shoes I find in the closet, and then I open the door to step out.

Right into the man's arms.

I stop in my tracks as he towers over me with the gun in one hand and a dead rabbit in the other.

With a gulp, I step back as he steps forward.

My cheeks flush as his eyes flash to the bag in my hands and the coat around my body. The closer he comes, the more I back away until I'm back inside his hut again, and the door closes behind him.

He clears his throat and hangs the rabbit on the same hook I took the coat from. But as he turns, his eyes bore into mine, and the fear pushes me back another step until I drop the bag in my hands.

He doesn't put down the gun.

"You were going to run ... weren't you?" he asks, his voice low and scratchy, like that of a psychopath, and it brings chills to my bones. "And here I was, thinking you were grateful."

"I-I am," I stutter, still moving backward.

Because that gun is still in his hands.

"That's a really strange way to show your thanks," he replies.

Sweat rolls down my back as I bump into the wall. "I'm sorry, I was just trying to—"

"Get away from that House?" he interjects. "Yeah, I know."

"I'm sorry," I mutter, hoping he'll forgive me for trying to steal his supplies.

The look on his face darkens. "Sorry's not gonna cut it."

My eyes widen.

"I'm gonna need something more than that."

I swallow, hoping this isn't going where I think it's going. "I don't understand."

"I think you do, girl ..." he says as he steps closer and closer until I have nowhere else to go. "Those boys back at the House want you back. And I told them you weren't here. Do you know what kind of risk I'm taking by lying?"

My body grows icy cold. That phone call ... it was all a lie.

He didn't rescue me to keep me safe.

He rescued me to use me for himself.

His hand reaches for my face, caressing my cheek. I shudder in place as tears form in my eyes. "I think I deserve something in return. And you need to prove to me that it was all worth it."

Bile rises in my throat as this disgusting man leans toward me. His hand slides down my neck as his eyes glide across my chest as though he's testing the goods to see if he likes them, and it sickens me.

Panic flushes my veins. "HELP!"

I've never screamed this loudly.

Suddenly, he grabs my throat and shoves me against the wall.

I try to yelp, but no sound comes out of my throat.

"Cheeky little girl," he growls. He pushes the gun against my chest, and I hold my breath. As tears roll down my face, he parts the coat with his gun until that silly flannel is revealed again.

"This once belonged to my wife ... I remember her wearing it on our honeymoon night as if it happened yesterday."

Oh God. I knew it, and still, I ignored the signs.

"Please ..." I whisper with what little breath I have left.

Suddenly, the door bursts open, and someone storms in. I'm choked to the point of barely being able to breathe, and I'm fading fast. My brain barely registers it when the guy shoving the gun against this flannel dress is dragged away, and his hands release from my throat.

I bend over and clutch my knees, coughing and heaving. It's only when I look up that I realize who just came in.

Soren.

The guy who barely spoke has come to beat the shit out of the guy keeping me here for his own pleasure.

How did he get here so fast?

Never mind, it's not important. No time to waste.

I have to run before he tries to take me back to Eli ... because that's exactly why he came to look for me.

While the two men fight, I grab the bag and throw it over my shoulder. I can't get past them yet, as they block the only route. But I'm watching, waiting for my opportunity. The gun goes off.

I cover my ears and squeal in panic. The bullet ricochets across the wood and exits through the roof.

A hatchet hangs on the wall next to the rabbit on the hook, and Soren snatches it off. With a loud grunt, he attacks the man and buries the hatchet in his arm. The man howls in pain, and I can't help but stare in complete shock as Soren butchers him. The arm with which the man was holding the gun drops to the floor as he shrieks in pain.

Then Soren focuses his eyes on me.

Adrenaline floods my veins, forcing me to act.

I jump sideways along the body as Soren leans over. Right then, the guy beneath us reaches for the gun with his other hand, causing Soren to fall while he tries to grab me. I barely manage to escape his grasp and make my way to the door.

I can't help but throw one final glance over my shoulder at the two men still fighting over life and death. Even though Soren came to my rescue and saved me from that horrible man's clutches, I can't let him catch me.

So without looking back again, I run.

# FIVE

## Eli

I'm going through every bottle of liquor in the kitchen cabinets, and still, I'm left with an unquenched thirst. No amount of drinking can ease the pain inside my heart, not even this headache banging my head into a pulp.

Something slams open, and I look up from my glass in a half-drunken haze. More noise ensues, and I'm starting to wonder whether I'm dreaming it all up or if someone's breaking into my house.

Soren suddenly bursts into the kitchen, dragging a body in his hands with a bloody trail behind him. My brow rises. "Interesting."

He throws the body on the floor in front of the door. I haven't seen that guy in a long time. A guard stationed on the mainland, east of the island, to act as both a safe keeper and a watcher. Now, he's missing an arm. I guess he's failed his job.

Soren is covered in blood, his breath heavy, his body covered in bruises. They were in a fight.

My nostrils flare.

"He had her, didn't he?"

He nods.

I take another big shot glass, fill it up, and chug it down in one go. "I'm glad you killed him. Or I would've gone over there and done it myself."

The mere thought of that swine trying to hide her from me fills me with rage. Whatever he'd planned to do with her can't have been good. If he tried to have his way with her, I would've cut off his dick and fed it to him personally.

But I guess it's too late for small joys now.

"I assume she's escaped again, seeing as you didn't bring her back?" I put down my glass.

He nods again.

My eyes narrow. "Figured."

I get off my seat and march toward him.

He stares me down, then throws a glance at the guy lying in his own bloody pool on the floor.

"Get rid of him. Erase any trails and wipe him out of existence completely," I say.

Soren sucks in a deep breath, then nods.

I pass him by and go directly into my study, ogling that one book that always makes me feel like my father's eyes are still boring into mine. I swallow and take it off the shelf, flipping to the last page where Amelia's name and everything important about her is written.

I flip to the next page and write down my wishes and vows.

Right then, Tobias walks in. "Did Soren—"

"No," I respond as I draw a knife from my drawer.

Tobias eyes the knife as I bring it toward my hand.

His eyes widen. "What are you ... are you making the vow?" I nod, and his eyes darken. "You can't do this. She's gone, you know that."

"I'll get her back," I say through gritted teeth.

Tobias marches toward me. "Do you have any idea what the repercussions are?"

"Don't school me. I know full well what I'm doing," I say, but as the knife nearly punctures my skin, he grabs my wrist.

"You're drunk," he growls. "I can smell it."

"And you think that's going to stop me?" I growl back.

"You're not thinking clearly," he retorts.

"I've never thought more clearly in my life," I say through gritted teeth. "She belongs with me."

"Even if that's true, are you willing to bear the consequences of your choice?" he asks. "We only get to choose once. So choose wisely."

"My parents were the embodiment of a failure," I growl, and I jerk my wrist back. "I know better than anyone what it will cost me."

"And still you're willing to go through with this?" he says, eyeing me down. "You know you're going to have to bring her back now, no matter the cost."

I pierce my skin with the blade, looking away as I make the cut. The blood is warm as it oozes down my skin, right onto the page.

"Yes, she will become my wife," I say, with my head held high as I splatter the last bit of blood onto the page.

Tobias never takes his eyes off me as he grabs the House Seal and smashes it onto the page.

"Fine. Have your wish," he says begrudgingly. "But as your advisor, I must add: Don't say I didn't warn you."

I nod. "Duly noted."

"Sir, I have—" Mary suddenly bursts into the room, but the second she spots my bloody hand and the rulebook, her jaw drops. "I—"

"Spill it," I growl, quickly covering my hand with a bandage I found lying in my drawer.

She refocuses her attention on me. "The helicopter has arrived."

"Finally," I reply, and I immediately barge past both of them. "I'll go find her myself."

\*\*\*

## Amelia

It takes me an hour to find a road and another to finally catch a passerby vehicle and hitchhike to a city. From there, it doesn't take me long to find others willing to drive me around for a little while until I finally get back to my hometown.

The familiar buzz of the city, the people walking about, the rain pitter-pattering down gently, it all brings me a kind of calm that nothing else can. But the minute I spot my apartment building, it suddenly becomes hard to breathe again.

A tear runs across my cheeks as I place my hand on the outside wall.

I didn't think I'd ever be back here. All this time spent locked up in a room, I dreamed about it, but I never thought it'd actually become a reality. That I'd actually escape and find my way back.

I go inside and walk up the familiar staircase until I get to my door. But I realize I don't have a key. Eli took it, along with all my other belongings, even my phone. And I never got a chance to take any of it back.

Taking in a big breath, I turn around and make my way to my landlord, who lives just one story up. Maybe he can help me out. I know I haven't been here for a very long time, and that rent has probably been due many times, but if I explain my situation ...

*He's going to call the police ... Who will come and check my apartment for the body of a missing guy.*

Chills run down my spine.

*I don't want to go to jail.*

Still, I have to try for the sake of my own sanity. To truly get all of my memories back, I have to see straight into my own past.

I sigh out loud as my hand hovers near his door. Then I knock.

The guy opens up within a minute, and the look on his face speaks volumes.

"Amelia?"

"Hi," I reply awkwardly.

"I thought you were—Oh my God, where've you been?" he asks.

I blush. "Um ... it's hard to explain."

"Ahh ... of course," he says, clutching the door.

"Sorry, I just ... is my apartment still available?"

He frowns. "Well, it was, but you didn't pay the last few times I asked for rent, and you were never there, so I put it up online as available for renting."

My lips part. "Oh ..."

*Of course, why didn't I think of that?*

He clears his throat. "But if you pay me tomorrow, I can give the apartment back to you."

I look away briefly, ashamed of not being able to pay

him what he's due. "No, I'm sorry, I can't."

"I understand," he says, nodding.

"But I will pay you back," I quickly say. "I promise, I will pay back what I owe you."

He nods a few times, and the conversation grows stale.

"I just ... wish I could visit the apartment one last time. You know, for old time's sake," I say, adding a gentle smile. "I never actually got to say goodbye."

He narrows his eyes. "Something bad happen to you?"

I look down at my feet, unsure of how to answer. I wish I could tell someone what happened to me, but to do so would put my own safety at risk. And that's just not worth it.

"I was just a little lost. That's all," I lie.

He just throws me this look but then sighs and releases the doorjamb. He fishes a key from his pocket and throws it at me. I barely manage to catch it in time.

"I'll need that back within three days," he says.

"Thanks," I reply, with a big smile on my face.

"Just don't make a mess of the place. I still need to get it refurbished."

"Of course," I reply, and I quickly take off before he changes his mind.

I go back to my apartment and stuff the key into the lock, but before I push open the door, I pause, lean in with my forehead against the wood, and breathe out.

*You can do this, Amelia. You can face your own worst nightmares.*

With a final breath, I go inside and close the door behind me.

The silence is murderous to the point that it makes me choke on my own oxygen. When I look into the kitchen, at the spot where I killed Chris, vivid images of his death flood my mind, and I can see my hand swinging that knife straight into his body.

My pulse begins to race.

I go to where his body is. Or where it should be.

Because it isn't there.

Along with all the blood … of which every speck has disappeared.

# SIX

*Amelia*

The day my whole life changed, I immediately went back home after I woke in a field in the middle of nowhere. But I didn't know back then what I know now.

I didn't know there was supposed to be a dead body on the floor, which somehow magically disappeared.

The whole thing still feels like such a blur. But the more time I spend here, the more the memories begin to seep back in.

I go to my knees and touch the floor where Chris's body once lay, but it's completely empty. The entire place is squeaky clean. As if he was never there to begin with.

And the knife … the knife that I stabbed him with is gone too.

The last time I saw it, Eli thrust it into the chair, and I used it to threaten him. I remember hearing the blade clatter to the ground. My hand rises to cover my mouth. If that was really the knife, my knife, then Eli must've taken it from this apartment.

Which means he was here.

Is that why Chris's body is gone?

My body feels weak, and my vision is blurry, so I grab the counter to steady myself. These memories continue to flood my brain, but I can't imagine myself actually killing someone. Would I even be capable of such a thing?

I shudder in place, thinking of all the reasons I had.

I hated Chris for using me. Betraying me. Lying to me. Hurting me.

Not just emotionally, but physically too.

\*\*\*

**Months ago**

"Why the fuck haven't you quit that damn job yet?" he shouts, picking up one of the miniskirts that I only wear at Joe's.

"Because I need to pay off my student loans. You know that," I reply, swallowing because I already know where this is headed. This always happens when he finally does come home, usually drunk.

He shrugs and chucks the skirt onto the couch as if it

means nothing to him. "Really? You can't just pay it off with the money you earn shuffling some books?" he scoffs.

I continue washing the dishes in the hopes that he'll cool off. "It doesn't pay much."

"Then get a better job," he yells in my ear, a little too close for comfort.

"No, I like it there," I reply.

The word *no* makes him glare at me as though I've set off a bomb.

"You know I don't like it when other men look at you," he growls, pointing at me. "So quit, or I'll call him myself."

"And then what?" I put down the glasses. "Who's going to pay off these loans? And what about the bills?"

He makes a face. "You'll figure something out. There are plenty of other jobs on the market, and I'm sure they're all dying for a pretty ditz they can use."

I frown. "Don't call me that. I'm not dumb."

"No?" Rage fills him up. "Then why do you work for Joe's? When the customers there treat you like shit?"

*Oh no. Here we go again.*

He grabs one of the glasses and shatters it on the ground.

"Goddammit, Amelia! Why can't you just do what I tell you?"

I don't respond. There's no point. Anything I say will only egg him on.

It's what he always does, how it always goes.

I'd just be adding spark to the fuel, and then we'll have a

raging fire.

"For once in your life, stop being a miserable little girl and do something you can be proud of! For fuck's sake!" he yells. "Look at what you made me do."

He points at the shards as if it's my fault he broke that glass.

Still, I don't want to argue with him, so I grab the broom and start cleaning it up.

"Really? So you're not even going to say anything?" He just stands there and watches me.

"Nothing I say will change your mind," I reply.

His nostrils flare, and when I look up, it's like he's lost all control. My eyes widen as he marches to the counter. I hold my arms up to protect my face as he picks up a plate and chucks it right at me. Luckily, it ends up on the ground, too, instead of smashing into me.

"Fucking hell, Amelia!" he screams. "Do something! Say something!"

But I can't.

I'm frozen to the ground, unable to move, to act ... unable to even defend myself. And I don't know why.

"I can't believe this," he says after a while, shaking his head. "What happened to making a better life for yourself after your parents died, huh? You were always crying about them."

"Don't bring my parents into this," I say, tears welling up in my eyes.

"Jesus Christ ..." Chris mutters, scratching his cheek

before marching off to the door. "Fuck this shit. I'm out of here. Go wallow in self-pity for all I care."

Before I can say another word, he slams the door behind him.

Two more plates tumble off the kitchen counter from the sheer force of the bang and shatter into a million tiny pieces.

Just as my heart does as I clean up the mess he made, wondering what I did to deserve this.

\*\*\*

**Present**

I always denied his abuse and told everyone who asked about my bruises that it was an accident. That I was clumsy and often fell. But that wasn't true, and I knew. I knew what Chris did to me, and I let him because I didn't want to face the consequences of what it meant. Of how weak I truly was.

Weak enough to want a man who didn't want me, who didn't need me, and who despised me just so I wouldn't feel alone.

I clutch my belly as the tears begin to flow. I don't want to acknowledge this pain gutting me, wrenching my heart into pieces.

Did I really hate Chris so much that I wanted him dead?

Me, a killer?

I stare at my hands which shake with fear.

Did these hands truly murder another human being?

Or did I imagine it all?

I close my eyes and force myself to think of something else before I'm lost in these thoughts.

I can't stay here. I have to get out.

It isn't safe.

Eli is going to look for me here. And if I know anything about him, it's that he won't give up the search. No, this is no place to stay for me.

So I get up and leave the apartment. Only one other place to go.

\*\*\*

# ELI

The helicopter's whirling blades normally set my heart at ease, but right now, it does the opposite. All I can think about is Amelia and how scared she must be all by herself. Especially after what she's been through. Soren told me about what that guard tried to do to her after lying to me about her being in his hut.

The mere thought of what he could have done to her sets fire to my already blazing heart. If I would've been there, I probably would've ripped his balls off and shoved them down his throat.

No one, absolutely *no one* gets to touch my Angel.

I'm glad Soren made him pay the price for his insolence.

I need to be more careful about who I hire. Double-check everyone's credentials and pay them triple for the effort to stay on the righteous path. They all know what they sign up for, and they should do their job as asked.

Grumbling to myself, I look out the window as I'm flown to my destination. I'm on my own now, but I will get her back. It's better this way with fewer distractions. Soren and Tobias need to stay behind anyway and look after the girls so they don't rebel. Although I'm not even sure anymore if that won't happen regardless of whether they're there, seeing as Amelia's escape happened right underneath our noses.

I can't let it happen again. I must bring her back and make her mine ... forever.

She will become my wife, and together, we will make sure the sinners are punished ... and my line will be continued.

A man and a woman, side by side, ruling over my family's House.

As it should have been.

\*\*\*

**Sixteen years ago**

"I'm done. Do you hear me? Done!"

My mother's voice echoes down the hallways. I can hear her from all the way here in my room. I don't need to see her to know that tears are running down her cheeks right this very moment.

And I don't need to be there to know what's going on.

"Daria, please," my father says.

"No. Let go of me!" she shrieks.

I look around to see if the guards are watching before rushing out of my room and across the hallway to where my father and mother are having a heated discussion in the living room.

She's standing over the balcony while he is right behind her, trying in vain to grasp ahold of her.

"Don't come near me, or I'll do it," she hisses at him, her back against the banister.

"Don't even try," my father growls.

"I can't take it anymore!" she screams, leaning dangerously over the edge.

Then her eyes meet mine, and she pauses.

My father tries to grab her arm. "Stop this nonsense right now."

"No," she barks back, focusing on my father again and swatting him away. "I don't care what you do anymore. I've tried to make sense of it, to see your ways, but I can't. You never stop hurting people. You're the one who needs punishment, not them."

It's not the first time I've heard her scream. But it's the first time she's actually done it in front of me.

"This is what we do here. You've known that for a long time," he says.

"But I never agreed!" she shrieks. "And you never even tried to see it from my perspective."

"It has to be done," he says, his posture rigid and unmoving, as though he's already given up.

"Then you can do it on your own. I'm done playing your games. I'm done trying to wait for the day that will never come," she says, and she hoists herself up the balcony's railing.

My eyes widen, and I gasp in shock.

My father steps forward. "Daria, stop this nonsense right now. We have a son together."

"I don't care!" she yells into the void. "You tricked me into this."

I'd be lying if I said it didn't hurt me, just like all the other times she's said it before.

"You knew what you were getting yourself into," he says, grasping her ankle. "There is no scrambling out of your choice."

She glances at him over her shoulder. "This was never my choice. It was yours," she hisses, then she glances at me. "Even having *him*."

Tears well up in my eyes. I wish I didn't care like she does, but I do. I wish I could unhear what she's saying, unsee the things she's doing, but it's impossible.

My father turns sideways, his eyes catching mine. And it feels, if only for a moment, as though I'm on fire.

"I don't love you. I never have." Her lips curl up as mine curl down. I don't know if she's speaking to my father … or to me. "You use him to keep me here. To force me to stay. But I am done living this lie. I'd rather not live at all," she says. And as the tears stream down her face, she attempts the jump.

My father catches her just in time, her body hanging by a simple grasp of his fingers around her ankle. But he refuses to let go, even when she begs him to.

Because they are married.

Because my father needs her to continue his House.

Our house.

The house that will one day become mine to rule … Over a pile of blood and bones.

# SEVEN

*Amelia*

**Present**

"Are you really sure I can stay?" I ask as I put down my stuff on Jamie's table. "I don't want to get in your way."

"Oh no, it's no problem," she says, waving it off as if it's no big deal. "You're not getting in my way at all."

"But I won't be able to pay this back," I add, swallowing down the shame. "At least, not until after I've gotten a job."

She glares at me from the kitchen. "And?"

A blush spreads across my cheeks. I don't even know how to respond to her generosity. "T-thank you," I mutter.

"Thank me after you're back on your feet." She winks. "So … do you want milk or sugar in your coffee?"

"Neither, please," I reply, wearing a big smile on my face. "Honestly, I can't thank you enough for letting me stay here."

"What else are friends for?" she says, putting two cups of steaming hot coffee down on the dining table. "Besides, I'd expect you to do the same for me if I was ever in trouble."

"Of course," I say. "Always."

She smiles as we sit down at the table. "So ... I don't mean to be nosy, but what happened?"

I look down at my cup and stare at the swirling coffee, wondering how I'm going to explain. "Ah ... Chris and I had an argument. I just couldn't stay there any longer. I ran, and ... well, I've been on and off the streets." It's a little bit of truth but with a lot of lies in it. And I hate having to do that, but what choice do I have?

"Oh, honey, you should've come to me sooner. I would've helped," she says, putting down her coffee cup.

I look away, ashamed of lying when she's so generous. "I was just really, really scared."

"I can only imagine," she says, her voice full of worry.

"It'll be fine once I get back on my feet," I say, trying to ease the tension. "Is ... is my job at the library still available?"

She makes a face and smashes her lips together, then shakes her head. "I'm sorry."

I nod a few times. "Figured."

"They needed to fill the spot as soon as possible. It was

too much of a workload for a single person," she adds.

I rub the back of my neck. "Oh yeah, I totally understand."

"But what about your bank account? Can't you access that to get some cash at least?" she asks.

I don't know how to respond. What do I tell her? That some crazy sin-obsessed billionaire is keeping all my accounts and my phone hostage until I return to be his pet again? No, this lie sounds more credible than that story.

"Chris ..." I mutter.

"Wow."

"It's just been very rough." I don't want to divulge too much information. I'm afraid she might force me to go to the police, and I can't tell them the truth either.

"And he's hogging your apartment all by himself?" She makes a tsk sound. "I shouldn't be surprised. He always seemed like an asshole to me. But I never really knew just how much."

"I know." I roll my eyes even though I know it's not the whole truth. "I should've realized he was bad for me a long time ago."

She reaches out and grabs my hand. "Honey ... When we're in the dark, we just don't see the light. That's just how it is. But you still managed to get out, and you should be proud of yourself."

"Yeah, but at what cost?" I sigh. "My home, my money ... my job."

I take a sip of the coffee to hide my own panic.

"Well, there must be something we can do. You could go to the police," she says.

"No."

My swift response makes her raise her brows.

"I just don't want to have anything to do with him anymore," I add. "I can't. I just can't do it."

Her face softens. "Oh, honey …"

I put down my coffee. "I wish I didn't have to make the choice …"

"You did what you had to do," she says, and she squeezes my hand tight. "You did it to protect yourself."

We have a moment together when suddenly the door opens. A little girl of about eleven years old enters the apartment and takes off her coat before she sees me, which is when she abruptly stops moving.

"Mimi, this is Amelia. She'll be staying with us for a while," Jamie says, cocking her head to look at the girl. "C'mon. Say hi."

I get up and smile at the girl when she approaches me cautiously, clutching her fingers together while tapping her feet. "Hi, Mimi. Nice to meet you."

"Hi," she says with a cutesy high voice.

"I'm a friend of your mom," I add.

"A friend? Mom rarely has friends over," she says.

Jamie's cheeks flush, and her brows rise. "That's not true."

"Yes, it is," Mimi says straight to her face, which makes Jamie shut her eyes in embarrassment.

"Okay, whatever you want. Just go do your homework," she says.

"Can I have some juice first?" she asks.

"Of course," Jamie says, sighing as she gets up from her seat and goes into the kitchen. "Here's a cookie too. Now go and do your homework quietly, okay? Mommy and Amelia have to talk."

"About what?" Mimi asks, and I hide my laughter behind my hand.

"Adult stuff," she replies. "Oh, and I want you to clean your room. Amelia will be sleeping in your bed tonight, and you'll sleep with me."

"MOM!" she retorts with her hands propped on her hips.

"Oh, no, you don't have to do that," I interject with a half-smile. "I'll sleep on the couch."

"The couch?" Jamie frowns at me as if I just suggested something truly insane.

"It's fine," I say as I pick up my coffee and move to the couch to pat it a few times. "I'm sure it's very cozy."

Jamie raises her brows at me. "Are you sure?"

I throw her a look. "Yes, this is perfect."

I honestly don't want to force a kid her age out of her own bed. She needs the independence.

"See, Mom? I can sleep in my own bed," Mimi responds, pursing her lips. "I'm not a baby anymore. Babies sleep with their moms."

Jamie rolls her eyes, which makes me laugh. "All right,

fine."

"Yay! See ya. Time for homework," Mimi says, as she quickly rushes to her room and shuts the door.

"No TV until you've finished!" Jamie yells after her, but there's no response, of course.

"She seems like a handful," I jest.

"Oh, you don't even know the half of it." She sinks into her chair and grumbles to herself. "These prepubescent hormones are giving me hemorrhoids."

I snort-laugh and almost choke on it. "Sorry."

"Oh, laugh away. I do it all the time. Keeps me from going insane," she says, twirling her finger around her temple.

"Must be hard, raising her all by yourself," I say, still seated on the couch.

"Yeah ... It's been rough since Paul died," she replies. "But I manage."

I nod a few times, unsure of what to say. It sounds rough to lose the man you thought you'd raise your daughter with. Now she's on her own with no one to help her. We're kindred spirits, stuck in the same kind of survival state that not many people understand.

But even if we can find a little bit of solace in each other's comfort by talking, I know I won't be able to stay. And to pay her back for all this, I'm going to have to find a job. Tomorrow.

\*\*\*

That night, Eli comes into the living room. Before I can scream, his hand has already covered my mouth. Our eyes lock as my body goes numb against the couch. Adrenaline floods my veins as he whispers, "Why? Why did you run, little Angel?"

I want to answer, but his hand still blocks my mouth.

"Is knowing the truth so bad?" he asks. "Do you wish I would just disappear so you could go back to your old life? To Chris?"

He leans in, his body against mine as I struggle to even breathe.

"Did you hate it so much to be with me?" he says, lowering his hand so my mouth is freed. But still, no sound can come out of my mouth. It's as though my lips are sewn shut, even when they aren't, but it feels like it … because I cannot utter a word when I look into his devilish eyes.

His face is so close to mine that I can feel his breath on my skin. "Is this what you want? To be away from me?" he whispers. "Say it then … say it out loud."

I gasp as his lips land on my neck, leaving a hot trail of desire, and I find myself grasping for the blanket around me, wishing it didn't feel so good. But as his tongue dips out and licks me all the way up to my chin, I can't help but close my eyes and let the lust rush inside and take me over.

Even if I wanted to, I can't say the words out loud.

I can't tell him to leave, even when I know I should.

Because I want nothing more than for his lips to be on

mine and for his hands to caress my body. For his greed to overtake mine. For my mind to become numb and forget everything and anything that was ever in my way. Even when it's wrong. Even when we are wrong.

"I want you," he whispers against my lips. "Tell me you want me too."

But when my lips part, no words can escape. Nothing ... except a sweet and delectable moan.

And when his lips capture mine, I am his.

Suddenly, my eyes burst open ... And Eli is gone.

Vanished, as though he was never even here.

And the dark of night has been replaced by the light of day.

My fingers hover close to my lips, a simple touch feeling like electricity jolts through my veins. Within the snap of a finger, I was no longer kissing him ... but I can still feel his lips on mine. And I can still feel his hands on my body, his weight bearing down on me, while my legs clenched together as the wetness began to flow.

*Fuck.*

*I really have fallen for him.*

I swallow hard and look around. The apartment still seems empty. Quiet as a mouse. Jamie nor her daughter Mimi are awake. Nothing in the apartment seems out of place, not even the door is open.

*But Eli ...*
*Eli was here. I was right here. He was kissing me.*
*Was it all a dream?*

I sigh out loud and rub my eyes, trying to make sense of it all.

Are my dreams that vivid? Or is his face just stuck in my head along with every little kiss he could ever give me?

Even thinking about it now, the way his mouth latched onto mine like he was desperate to have me, like he'd do anything for it, makes me feel as if I'm floating on air. But I shouldn't be, and I know that. He is bad for me, even when he makes me wish he was really here.

With a groan, I throw the blanket off, forcing myself to forget that I liked kissing him, and that I was secretly turned on. There's no time for stupid dreams and wishful thinking.

I have to find a job as soon as possible and get the fuck out of here. I can't stay here, even if I want to, even if Jamie tells me it's okay. Because she doesn't know what kind of danger she's in. She doesn't know he could be here at any moment to take me back.

And she needs to stay safe.

So I put on my clothes, grab my stuff, write her a note that I'm going to work and pay her back, and leave, determined to pay her back for her generosity some other time.

# EIGHT

## ELI

After the helicopter landed, I immediately got into the rental car and went to her apartment. Of course, she wasn't there. But I did manage to talk to the landlord and confirm she had been there.

So I went straight toward the second place she might be: her workplace. The only safe spot she's ever known. But when I get there, the only face in front of the desk belongs to her coworker.

"Can I help you?" the woman asks.

"Is Amelia here?" I ask, trying to remain calm.

The woman furrows her brows at me. "Sir, this is a library. Do you need help?"

So she's going to play hardball with me. Fine. I slam my fist on the desk. "Tell me where she is."

The woman leans back in her chair as far away from me

as she possibly can. "I don't know what you're talking about."

"I think you do," I retort, glaring at her.

She raises her brow at me. "I think you need to leave."

"You've seen her, haven't you?" I bark. "You know where she is. You just won't tell me."

She merely stares me down, but her eyes are twitching, and her nostrils flare. She's getting suspicious. "Who are you?" she asks after a while.

Grinding my teeth, I turn around and march off. I can't risk her calling the police. Not when I'm so close to hunting her down. If she refuses to answer, that means she knows Amelia might be in danger, which means they've talked.

She has to be close.

I can sense it.

All I need to do is reach out and grasp.

*But where ... where could she be?*

Then it hits me.

The club where I first discovered her dark edge, the one where I told her to stop working and leave. Maybe she hasn't listened after all.

\*\*\*

# Amelia

"Are you sure?" I ask.

"Yes, now get out of my way. I have customers," Joe barks, quickly shoving past me.

I sigh out loud and stare at the other waitresses bustling about with drinks and snacks while the customers gleefully gaze at the luscious women twirling away on the stage.

Even here, there is no more place for me.

One of the ladies in the back has my tables already. I've been replaced, and there's nothing I can do about it, nor do I blame Joe. Of course he'd find someone else. His business needs to be kept running. And the last time he saw me here, I fled the scene without ever coming back. I'd probably do the same if I was in his position.

Sighing, I throw one last look at the place before I call it quits and walk out the grimy old door. I don't think I'm going to come back here again. Sometimes things are just not meant to be. Besides, I don't have the best memories here. Every other day, we'd encounter a grabby customer or a complete drunk who'd refuse to leave and give us trouble. Just like what happened last time I was here … when Eli found me and held a gun to that asshole's head. The thought of which still gives me the chills.

I shake it off as I walk away from the dank building.

Wretched smells from the side alley's dumpsters fill my nostrils and make me want to hurl, but my stomach is easily put to rest by the sheer look one of Joe's customers gives me as he drinks up a whole bottle of whiskey right beside the door.

"Well … well … hello there, pretty girl," he murmurs, completely intoxicated. "Where are you going?"

I don't respond. I just keep walking until I'm as far away from the dude as possible.

Unfortunately, that doesn't help to keep him at bay.

"C'mon, where are you going?" he shouts. "Tell me!"

"Leave me alone!" I yell over my shoulder.

The sickening smile that follows makes the hairs on the back of my neck stand straight.

"Don't walk away from me," the guy barks as my pace increases.

The sun has already set, and there aren't many people on the streets to blend in with.

How am I going to get rid of him?

My pulse is racing as adrenaline rushes through my veins. I need to shake him off fast. So I take a detour across town until I get to a particular busy bar strip with loads of customers, and I throw myself into the first bar I can find.

I disappear between the tables and the people talking to each other, who seem surprised by me being there, interrupting their fun. I pay no attention to their stares as I try to hide from the man searching for me. He's right outside, pacing around with that bottle still in his hands. My heart still beats in my throat while I peek at him from behind a customer.

After a while, he gives up and walks away, and I breathe a sigh of relief.

*Why was he so interested in me?*

*Was he one of Eli's henchmen?*

A shiver runs up and down my spine.

Suddenly, a hand touches my shoulder, and I jolt from the scare.

"Sorry, I just wanted to ask if you wanted to order a drink?" a waiter says.

"Uh … no, sorry," I reply, and I leave right away before I get into trouble here too.

I've had enough for today.

\*\*\*

# Eli

I storm into the club, not giving a shit about the stares the other customers give me. I'm not here for any kind of pleasure except to find the girl who belongs to me.

"Was she here?" I ask. "Amelia."

"Who? Amelia? I don't know—"

I grab his collar. "Yes, you do."

"Hands off, fucker," he growls.

As his bodyguards step forward, I pull out a gun.

"You don't want to mess with me," I growl, pointing it at them. "Now tell me if she was here."

He holds up his hands. "Look, I don't want any trouble. She was here to ask about her job."

My nostrils flare. "Is she here *now*?"

"No, I didn't need more waitresses. I don't know where she is now. She left through that door." He points at the one in the back.

I put him down on the floor again. "Jesus, thanks." He throws his bodyguards a look. "Now get out before I call the cops."

"No fucking need. You should be happy I'm not here for you," I growl back, and then I turn around and barge out.

I'm not in the mood to start some more trouble even though I know this guy definitely deserves it with how he treats these women who work for him.

But I have more important things to do right now … like finding my little angel and making sure she's safe, so I can whisk her back into my world and make her stay.

It's where she belongs, by my side, like it was always meant to be.

And I think I know where she's run off to.

\*\*\*

## Amelia

Rubbing my arms to fight the cold, I go back to the only place I know I can go; my apartment. Even though the place isn't mine anymore, I have nowhere else to go. Going back to Jamie's would mean risking her life, not to mention her little daughter. I just can't do that to her.

So I walk all the way back to the building I once lived in, to the apartment where my life was destroyed. And I go up the stairs to my floor, hesitating for a moment before I open the door. Even now, it still brings chills to my bones.

Despite the fact there is no body and no evidence of what I did.

I clutch the doorjamb, staring at the remains of my life. I have nothing left. Nothing to hold. Nothing … except that man who haunts even my very own dreams. Who showed me the truth I thought I wanted to know until I stared it right in the face and saw how vicious I truly was. Who, out of all people, I now miss the most.

I snort out loud, which quickly turns into a cynical laugh as I sink to the floor. Things can't get much worse than this. But the worst part of it all is that I know I deserve it … because Chris is gone, thanks to me.

At least, that's what I remember. I killed him … but there's no trace of him left, which makes me wonder if my memories can even be trusted at this point, especially with everything that's happened.

Suddenly, someone sauntering into the hallway catches my eye. It's a guy with a bottle of whiskey in his hand. The same drunk who followed me from that alley ... now followed me home.

Panic floods my veins as I scramble up from the floor as fast as possible, but not fast enough to stop the guy from chasing after me and blocking my door with his foot so I can't close it.

I squeal as he barges inside, slamming the door open wide.

"You thought you could run from me?" the guy yells, slurring every other word. "I like a bit of a challenge."

"Get away from me!" I scream, crawling across the floor.

He laughs. "You think a tiny mouse like you could scare me off?" He steps closer, taking a big gulp of his bottle before chucking it aside on the floor. "I think I'm going to have a bit of fun with you."

I shake my head as I turn around on my knees and try to get up. But his body lands on top of mine, squashing me instantly, almost making it impossible for me to breathe.

"No!" I shriek when he tugs at my pants.

His disgusting breath smells of alcohol as he whispers into my ear. "C'mon, show me what you've got to offer."

Tears well up in my eyes as I gasp for air.

Suddenly, the guy is torn away from me, and I can

breathe again.

I turn around on my back and look up, only to lose my breath entirely at the sight of the man pounding away on the drunk.

Eli.

# NINE

## Eli

Indescribable anguish fills my bones when I spot someone else trying to take what's mine. I lash out in fury, roaring out loud while tearing him off her with almost inhumane strength. I grasp him by the collar and lift him, only to punch him right in the jaw.

"What the fuck?!" the guy squeaks. His breath stinks of alcohol.

"STAY THE FUCK AWAY FROM HER!"

I kick him in the gut so hard I lose grip, and he falls to the floor.

An oompf sound leaves his mouth. "Fuck…"

I kick him again and again until he cries out in pain. "I'm sorry!"

"Should have thought of that before. You. Tried. To. Use. Her." Each syllable uttered is another kick to the stomach until he coughs up blood.

Then I pull the gun from my holster and hold it over his head.

"Now say a prayer," I growl.

"No, wait!"

Amelia's high but dangerously loud voice makes me stop in my tracks and focus on her as she gets up from the floor. Salty tears stain her round, pink cheeks, and I wish more than anything that she wouldn't have to cry them. Tears he put there. And I wish that she wouldn't have to pout with those sweet, red lips so desperately that it tugs at my heartstrings. And I'm torn between wanting to wrap her in my arms and murdering this son of a—

"Don't do it," Amelia says, upending my train of thought.

"He has to be punished for his sins," I respond, my voice shaky, unruly, as though it's coming unhinged at the seams, just like I am when I look at her in all her misery and sorrow that I wish I could erase.

And the only way to do that is to erase him from this planet.

I redirect my attention back to the drunk and pull the safety off the gun. The guy pisses his pants. "Please. Please. *Please*, don't kill me." His eyes are closed, and his entire body is shivering. "I'm sorry, I'm so sorry. I promise I won't ever do it again. Please, let me go."

"No … you won't," I say through gritted teeth, pointing my gun straight at his forehead.

Suddenly, Amelia grabs my arm, and I'm torn between this drunk who dared to touch her and the woman I want to hold in my arms and never let go. Even with tears staining her eyes, she still clings on to a life that doesn't belong to her.

"Eli, stop," Amelia says with a soft but outspoken voice.

"Why?" I ask, grinding my teeth. "Why should I stop?"

"Not every crime deserves death," she replies.

"This one certainly does." I know she can see the rage spilling out of me, but it's hard to keep it in when I've fought so hard to finally get to her only to watch her crumble in front of me because of someone else's actions. I can't let this go. I just can't.

But as my eyes flutter back to the drunk lying in front of me, my finger hovering over the trigger, she goes to stand between him and me, her arms and legs wide.

*How? How could she defend this man?*

"I don't understand," I say, my hand shaking because shame is flooding my system at the thought of pointing a gun to her chest. "Amelia. Why would you want this man to live after what he did to you?"

"Because everyone deserves a second chance. And no one else needs to die because of me," she says, keeping her head held high, despite the fact the man she's protecting is a monster who tried to use her innocence against her.

"Even *him*?" I growl.

"Even him." A tear rolls down her face. "Because if he doesn't get one ... how could I deserve one?"

Her words undo me. They crack what was left of the protective barrier I'd constructed around my heart. And as her hand rests on my arm, I let her lower the gun until it's no longer pointed at anyone, and my heart is no longer screaming for me to kill this man who dared to defile her.

Because when she wraps her arms around me, everything around us ceases to exist.

\*\*\*

## Amelia

"Thank you," I mumble.

The words fall from my mouth with ease even though I know Eli isn't a good guy. He protected me. All that anger, all that rage, confounded into one single thing … love. And that made him fight for me. How can I not be grateful?

Behind us, the drunk's feet drag across the floor as he pulls himself up.

"Fuck you, I'm out of here," he growls, but I pay no attention to him.

All I can do is bask in the warmth of Eli's body, his intoxicating scent filling my nostrils, pulling me in closer and closer until I want nothing more than for him to stay.

He saved me from a fate I wouldn't wish on my worst

enemy. And not just that. When I was down on my knees, crying, wishing I wasn't alone, wishing he was here … he actually came. And I don't know why, but my heart beats faster and faster when I hear his. With my head against his chest, I want nothing more than to stay like this, for all eternity if I could.

But I know that isn't possible.

Because he is the man who kept me as a prisoner.

I pull back, taking a few steps away from him. The drunk is already gone. All that's left is him and me. Us. And all the millions of unspoken words we have yet to say.

His lips part as he gazes at me, and mine do too, but I can't find the words for the thoughts swirling through my head. All the questions were left unanswered. All the reasons for my escape. All the lies that led to my betrayal.

"That was brave of you …" he murmurs after a while.

My fists clench. I thought about hurting that man. I wanted Eli to pull the trigger so badly, but I knew it wasn't right. That man was awful, and he deserves to be punished for what he did, but he didn't deserve to die.

"I did what I had to do," I say as images of his gun flash in front of my eyes again. "To make you stop."

He frowns, his posture rigid, like a rock. "Is that what you want? For me to stop?"

I swallow as an unsettling feeling grows in my stomach. "If it will make people stop hurting, then yes."

"I'm not the one who causes the hurt," he says, his face darkening.

When he steps closer, I step away. Even when I know I cannot trust him, I still sense a kind of disbelief. Like I wish it would be different.

"Why did you run?" he asks.

"You know why," I hiss.

"No," he says. "And to be frank, I was upset when you left without telling me."

I snort. "You think I'd tell you that I was going to run? After how the first escape went?"

He sucks in a breath loudly. "Your punishment wasn't over yet when you first ran."

"Oh, and now it is?"

He blinks a couple of times and looks away. "You remember your sin now."

I sigh, biting the inside of my cheek as I hate that he's reminded me of Chris. "That doesn't change a thing."

"Yes, it does," he says, and when our gazes connect once again, I'm almost blown away by the sheer fire in his eyes.

"No!" Tears well up in my eyes. "Me remembering what I did, doesn't change the fact that Chris is still gone."

He makes a face. "Do you miss him?"

"Yes, no, argh!" I pace around the room until I stop in the middle and just glare at him. "Why does this have to be so confusing?"

"Because emotions are complicated," he says. "They always have been."

"I don't need your lecture," I retort. "I just want all of

this gone. Gone! Do you hear me?"

"Amelia." He offers a hand, but I ignore him. "I can't take the memories away."

"You brought them back!" Tears flow freely down my cheeks. "Take them back! I don't want them!" I shove him aside when he tries to approach me. "No, get away from me."

"Amelia—"

"No!" I've finally found my voice. I won't let myself be walked over again. That's what I've always done. Well, not anymore. "You had that knife. *My* knife. I can't trust you."

"I already told you, I got it—"

"From here!" I fill in for him. "So you came into my apartment *after* I had killed him. Why? How did you even know I was here?" I swallow hard. "Were you the one who got rid of his body?"

He nods, and my insides knot together.

His face suddenly softens. "When you were out on your birthday, I followed you home. I waited and then saw what happened through the window. When I went up there, you were already gone. That's when I found Chris stabbed, not breathing."

I choke on my own breath.

"So I called in some favors and had his body removed, and the place cleaned up."

"Why?" I say through gritted teeth, my voice getting more and more unsteady by the second.

"Because I needed to save you from yourself," he says.

"Because I couldn't let you do that to yourself. After all you'd been through, for all the pain he made you suffer." He sighs. "You didn't deserve to go to jail."

I can't fucking believe this.

All this time, I thought I was going insane, but it was him. He cleaned up the body, taking Chris away so I never had to see him again ... I didn't have to see what had become of me.

But at what price?

"One last thing," I mutter, ignoring the tears still running across my cheeks and the pang in my stomach as I try to shove aside the feelings I have for him. "Did you know I was going to kill him?" I rub my lips together.

He doesn't reply, which tells me enough. But his face. God ... his face ... so full of misery and despair that it undoes me.

I shake my head. "I can't do this." And I run off into the hallway, down the stairs as fast as I can, as fast as my lungs and beating heart can go. Because if I stop ... what will become of me?

How could I accept these emotions for him, for this man who forced me to remember the very thing I wished I could forget?

So I run and run until my legs begin to shake. Until the sky above splits open and heaven itself punishes me with a downpour that douses any flames ignited in my heart.

\*\*\*

# ELI

I follow her outside toward the grass field, near the woods. Rain pitter-patters down onto us, but I pay no attention to the cold, despite it completely soaking my clothes through in mere minutes.

She stands there with slumped shoulders, staring down at the grass as though it holds a part of her soul. And it moves me to my core to see her like that. It makes me wish I could tear the pain out of her, mend her wound with my bare hands, and sew up the gaping hole so the scar would be almost invisible.

But I know that's not possible. I've seen it firsthand on my own skin, my very own sins that I carry with me on my back to this day.

"This is where I woke up … after I killed Chris…" Her words sound painful. Too painful to listen to. But I must.

I stand behind her, waiting for her to tell me what she really thinks. I know she knows I'm here, and even though our bodies don't touch, her shoulders still rise and stay that way, as though she can feel the electricity between us. "How did you know I was going to do it?"

"I was watching you. Ever since we met at the library," I reply. "I saw the bruises. And I knew the pain would become too much for you to bear."

She shudders, but I don't know if it's from the cold or

from my answer. "You were stalking me."

My nostrils flare. She's hit a chord. I've tried so long to deny it, to keep it hidden, but it's futile. I want her. I need her to be mine. I cannot stand being apart from her. Every second is too much. "Because I needed you to be safe. Because I needed *you* ..."

"But you didn't even know me," she scoffs, glancing at me over her shoulder.

"Yes," I say, swallowing hard. "Yes, I do."

She turns around, and we stare at each other for a moment. The silence is deafening, and my throat begins to clamp up.

"Do you remember that day you went to visit a funeral with your grandparents? They were old friends of my father. An urn of a young woman sat on the table there, and in front stood a boy you talked to?"

Her eyes widen. Pupils dilated. Skin turned white as snow. And while the rain scatters droplets across her skin, our seemingly separate worlds suddenly come crashing together.

Her lips part, rain and tears mixing together while they roll down her cheeks as one. Her hand rises, and I'm expecting a slap. Instead, it's the gentlest of touches that bring warmth in the frigid cold, setting my heart ablaze.

"It's you ... you were that boy, weren't you?" she murmurs.

I nod as I clutch her hand. "We met because we were supposed to. I knew then I was going to find you again. And

I did, thanks to that money your grandparents gave to our House as a gift."

Her lips part in shock. "So that's where the money went."

I frown and swallow, as my words have weighed heavily on me for a while. "I waited for a long time, but I couldn't stop thinking about you. The books my father kept were the only place I'd find a trace of your grandparents ... and with that information, I was finally able to track you down."

I tilt my head down. "That day, at my mother's funeral, you saved me from myself ... so I came to save you in return."

She swallows, visibly shaken, as though she too is contemplating what it means to love. What it means to hate. And all the complicated emotions between. And maybe, just maybe, we are both finally realizing what it means to be alive.

# TEN

*Amelia*

This silent moment in time feels like it lasts for an eternity. No matter how much I try, I can't look away from him, and neither can he.

As he stands there with his head between his broad shoulders, black suit completely wet, white shirt clinging to his abs, I finally see the truth. It's him, that boy with the solemn eyes. How could I not see that before?

All this time, I wondered why I felt as though I knew him, why it felt as though our worlds had entwined before. Why it felt like I wasn't merely a random choice that he made.

He's not just the man who stalked me, captured me, took me to his castle, and forced me to remember sins I wished I hadn't committed. He's also the boy drowning in sorrow and misery, as I was too a long time ago. And that same innocent boy and girl grew up to become monsters shaped by their own vision of the world and the people who lived there. Two sides to the same coin.

"I always felt like I knew you, somehow …" I mutter, my hand still on his face, unable to let go of the moment that feels so important, so precious. "Why didn't you tell me?" I ask.

I wish he would've told me about my grandparents being connected to all this. That they'd given this House the money they should've given me.

But I know I can't blame Eli either. After all, it was their choice to give that money away.

"I mean, not just my grandparents giving their money to your House but also the fact you already knew me before we met at the library?"

"I …" He looks away for a second, as though he's conflicted. "I didn't want to be seen as weak."

"Weak?" The way he says it, as though his heart is being twisted into knots, undoes me. I remember that boy standing in front of his mother's urn, wishing he was born into a different family. "No, you weren't weak. You were surviving through suffering."

His face contorts. "I despise my own history. I prefer not to talk about it."

"Is that the reason you want to punish others? Because of your own pain?" I ask.

"Perhaps." He sighs. "But it doesn't matter. What matters now is that I have you back safe and sound." He takes my hand off his face and presses a kiss to the top. "You were always my little angel."

*Angel? Me?*

Blood and stab wounds aren't caused by angels. They're the work of the devil.

I'm no more a saint than he is.

"Stop," I hiss, retracting my hand. "Stop calling me that."

He makes a face, seemingly confused. "Why?"

"I'm not an angel," I say. My body starts to shake, though I don't know whether it's from the coldness of the rain or the emotions laid bare. "I killed someone. Don't you understand?"

"Yes, I do," he replies.

My lips quiver as I gaze up into his deep, dark eyes hidden behind those thick lashes where raindrops fall as slow and hard as I do for him. But I can't let these emotions take control of me. Not when I finally realize all that I've done. All that's happened … because of him. "You made me do this. If it wasn't for you—"

"Then what?" he interjects as we have a stare down. "You would never have murdered him?"

The air between us is thick with tension.

"You would have stayed with him even though he hurt you, repeatedly?" He looks down at my lower leg, beneath my skirt, at the spot where the bruise used to be. Now there's nothing but pristine, pretty skin. I'm like a porcelain doll all patched up, but no amount of golden paint can brush up the scars lying underneath the surface.

And I am tired. Tired of having to erase my own history. Tired of having to fight for my own justice. Tired of trying to blame my own actions on others. Tired of having to face this constant battle between right and wrong, guilt, shame ... and relief.

No one is supposed to feel that way after the death of a loved one. Or at least ... someone you told yourself you should love. Someone who always said he loved you, even when his actions proved otherwise. But no one ever taught me what love truly is. How it shapes a person. What it makes them do.

All I know is the love of my parents vanished overnight. And the love my grandparents gave me never came close ... nor did it last long enough to matter.

\*\*\*

**Two years ago**

Leaves fall down upon the holes dug in the ground as my grandmother joins my grandfather in the grave. She only lasted a couple of months longer than he did. Her doctor said she died of a broken heart.

I don't think either of them was ready to die yet.

Not that it matters.

They're gone now, and I have no more family left.

All I can do is stare at the ground as the casket is lowered inside. Tears well up in my eyes as the sun shines brightly onto the wood. It shouldn't be such a beautiful day for such a sad occasion. Maybe this is my grandmother's way of saying a final goodbye.

Still, as she's hoisted in, I can't help but turn away and cry. The only one to console me is Chris, a friend who I met online and have been speaking to for quite some time. We've only met in person a few times before, but I still asked him to come because I didn't know anyone else, and I needed support.

How does one bury their last living relatives all by themselves?

It's impossible. So I turn to him, looking for him to console me even though he doesn't even know me that well. But when his arms wrap around me, I cry harder and harder against him, feeling like I can finally let out all the pain suffocating me since both of them died.

Even though I barely know this guy, he's still here, and that's what matters.

"C'mon. Let's get something to drink," he says after the ceremony is over.

And even though I wasn't ready to walk yet, I still let him whisk me away.

Out of misery … just so I can forget.

\*\*\*

**Present**

Death has been such an intrinsic part of my life that I believed it belonged there.

That it was a natural consequence of the pain we suffered.

That I, too, deserved death. Because why would I be alive and my parents and grandparents be dead?

"Why?" I mutter, unable to keep the tears at bay. "Why did I stay? Why didn't I fight? Why didn't I—"

Suddenly, his arms clasp around me, crushing me into his embrace. The warmth exuding from his chest overpowers the chills in my bones.

"You blamed yourself for all the pain in your life," he says. "Told yourself you deserved it. But you don't have to do that anymore."

Tears stream down my face like the rain poured down the crevice of the cliff my parents' car dived into. A never-ending flurry of knives stabbing my heart, making me want to howl from grief.

"All these years, I let him hurt me," I mutter, disgusted with myself. "How could I?"

"Because you wanted to feel loved," he says. "You were afraid of what it would mean when even someone like him couldn't love you …"

He's right. Chris didn't love me. He never did. And I fed myself lie after lie to make it so that it wasn't true. To make myself not feel alone in this world.

And I whisper the words I'd never dared to say out loud. "Why does everyone leave me?"

Fear strikes me down, making my knees buckle, but Eli doesn't move. He doesn't even flinch as he hugs me even tighter. How could he stay? How could he console a broken girl like me, a girl ruined by her own thoughts, a girl who hated the world she lived in so much she decided to destroy it?

"I'm here … and I won't ever leave you," Eli says. "No matter what."

"But I did. I ran away from you," I say, guilt eating away at me.

"It's okay," he says, silencing me. "I forgive you."

He was there for me, right when everything came crashing down. When I was at my lowest point, when I actually murdered another human being … he picked me up again and cleaned up my mess. And I forced myself to forget in order to numb the pain.

But I deserve better. I deserve to remember all the pain and suffering so that I won't ever let it happen to me again. I deserve to be loved, even after all the things I did. Even if I'm a sinner. And in Eli's arms, I find the solace I've so desperately been searching for.

"Now, let's go home," he says with a rugged voice that takes my breath away.

A squeal leaves my throat as he swoops me up into his arms.

"Home?" I mutter, confused as to what he means.

But he doesn't respond. Instead, he keeps his head held high as he marches right back to my apartment building and goes inside. Our bodies leave dripping wet marks on the carpet, but he pays no attention to it as we step into the elevator and ride it up to my floor.

For some reason, I can't stop staring at the handsome man, one I used to call a stranger, now a familiar face that I wish I could stare at all day long. How did it happen so fast? I didn't even know I was able to fall until he made me. Until he showed me who I truly am.

Not just a monster ... but a survivor. Someone who lives and breathes the pain they suffered carries it with them like a badge of honor. Does he do it too?

With my hands firmly locked around his thick, muscular neck, I let him carry me right back into what once was my home. It feels so strange to be back here with the man who took me away from this life. Like two completely different worlds are intertwining into a beautiful mesh.

He puts me down on the floor and goes into the bathroom, where he turns on the light and the shower. Then he walks to me again and places his hands on my waist. The second his hands touch my skin, I jolt up and down, an unexpected heatwave flashing through my body.

A quirky grin briefly brightens his face. "Take it off."

My cheeks turn crimson red as I realize what he's asking.

"You're soaking wet and shivering," he says.

And without taking his eyes off mine, he hooks his

fingers underneath my top and curls it up over my head, throwing it aside. My arms instinctively cover my breasts, even though he's already seen them. Before, I didn't want to hide ... but now I do. I don't want to hide my body ... I want to hide myself, my heart ... and the scorching hot flames coming off his eyes the minute he sees me undressed.

I didn't think it could affect me more than it already did, but I was wrong. Especially when his tongue dips out to swiftly wet his top lip.

I gulp when he goes to his knees in front of me and zips down my skirt from the back, sliding his hands inside only to push it down softly along with my underwear. He's so close to me when he lifts his face, and his eyes bore into mine. I've forgotten how to breathe.

And when he presses a soft, delectable kiss to my thighs, I die a little.

The kisses don't stop. And I don't pull away either as he draws a line from my thighs all the way up to my pussy, deeper and deeper until there's no way back. Until there's only him and me in this twisted, fucked-up nightmare that's beginning to feel more like a dream after all.

His tongue dips out to lick me, and I grasp the wall behind me, desperate for something to hold. Every stroke he adds is another one that makes me want more and more until I'm left gasping for air. His tongue twists and turns around my clit until a moan escapes my mouth.

He pauses and looks up, a gleeful smile on his face, and I realize at that moment that I have unequivocally fallen in love with this monster of a man.

"Don't ever hide from me." His dominant voice makes goose bumps scatter on my skin.

I don't get the chance to say a word because he dives back in, alternating licks and kisses until I'm delirious with need. My body is shivering, not from the cold but from pure pleasure, and I don't want it to stop. Screw us being wrong. If everything is so wrong, I don't want to be right anymore.

"Let me take your pain away," he whispers against my skin.

Delicious licks follow as he laps me up until I'm quivering in place.

"Please …" The word spills out of me. I didn't mean to beg, but his twisted tongue makes me want to sin. "More."

Even when my hand grasps his hair, he doesn't stop. And as his tongue circles around and dips inside me, I fall apart right then and there. My wetness gushes over him, and he keeps on licking me through the waves of pleasure until they subside.

"You look gorgeous when you come undone." He licks his lips as though he's just had dessert.

Suddenly, he whisks me up into his arms again and plops me down underneath the shower. Despite still being fully clothed, he turns it on, the hot stream of water landing right on his already wet chest. And my eyes can't help but gawk at the thick ridges of his abs clearly visible through his white tee. He steps closer. Water rushes down, droplets hanging on his lips just like I am.

"Kiss me," I mutter without thinking about it.

It's the only way to know for sure what it is that I feel. What *he* feels. If any of this means *anything*.

He swallows hard. Then he grabs my chin and lifts my face, planting his rugged lips onto mine for a sweet, delicate kiss that sets my heart on fire. I thought I could win, that I could fight this urge, but it's too late.

The second I kissed him, it was over, and I already knew this in my heart. I just couldn't face the truth ... that feeling I've been hiding from for so long. The one where I want nothing more than for him to take me, keep me, love me.

It's wrong. So wrong that I banished it to the back of my mind and forced myself to forget it.

But every time he touches me, kisses me, it lights this fire I can't ignore.

When our lips unlatch, I stare at him for a moment, hoping to find whatever it is that I'm looking for in his eyes, but they're filled with so many mixed emotions that I can't pinpoint what he's feeling, let alone what I'm feeling right now.

But within seconds, he's smashed his mouth right back onto mine.

Our kisses are greedy, senseless, and uncontrollable. Like fire and gasoline exploding under the water. I don't stop, and neither does he, even though I'm pretty sure this isn't what he's supposed to do as the man who punishes the sinners. But I guess I'm not the only one who's fallen beyond disgrace.

"I need you," he whispers against my lips. "I can't stop myself."

And I moan in delight as he parts my lips with his, shoving his tongue inside to lick the roof of my mouth. I'm struck by my own lust for him, for how badly I want him to shove me against the wall and fuck me until I'm begging to come.

Did he make me this way? Or was I always a vixen, and I just didn't know it yet?

But I can't even think about an answer because of his kisses and the way his hand snakes around my body to pull me close. I'm desperate for more as his other hand cups my face to kiss me even harder. He only stops to offer me a breath.

"Don't stop," I whisper, heady and drunk on his intoxicating love.

He smiles against my lips and gives me another peck. "Oh, believe me ... I'm only getting started."

Another kiss, and I'm fumbling at his pants until I've found the zipper and rip it all down. When his cock pops out, he groans out loud, the sound turning me on even more.

He lifts me in his arms and smashes me against the wall, and my legs wrap around his waist as he thrusts inside in one go.

My mouth forms an o-shape, but he swiftly covers my mouth with his, not letting an inch of my surprise go to waste. His hunger overtakes me, makes me give in so easily, even when I shouldn't.

Every thrust makes me want him closer, deeper, harder. Every kiss makes me wish he would never stop. Even when my brain tells me this isn't okay, that I shouldn't crave a man like him, my heart is desperate for his dirty love.

So I let him fuck me against the wall, again and again, pounding into me until our heavy breaths mingle, sweat mixing with hot water until he groans out loud. Until we're both lost in complete and utter debauchery, and nothing's left but lust and longing.

And when he explodes inside me, filling me up with his warmth, I come with him. Our bodies entwined, we stare into each other's eyes as we fall apart, not as captor and captive, but as equals. And for the first time in a long time, I feel as though I can take on whatever the world gives me … just by being in his arms.

His forehead leans against mine as he breathes out loud, his top lip hovering so close to mine that I can still taste him on my lips. I'm drunk on his kisses, drunk on our sex, wishing it would never end.

And my hands instinctively curl around his neck to toy with his hair as he gazes at me with those dark, hooded eyes from underneath his lashes. A gaze filled with so much adoration that it shatters the icy cage where I stored my frigid heart. One last kiss seals it.

Right then, my hand dives into his shirt, and I abruptly pull back. The skin on his shoulders is rugged and bumpy, like a rocky road, and I wonder why. It felt like … scars.

"What …?" I mutter as we gaze at each other, but the look on his face turns sour. He swiftly pulls back, causing my hand to drop off his shoulder.

"Don't," he says, adjusting his shirt even though it's wet and must feel uncomfortable.

"I wasn't—"

"I can't." He interrupted me, but not in a way that feels forced. More in a way that it hurts him to talk.

He swiftly pulls his pants back up and zips them, then turns around and walks out of the bathroom. Leaving me alone underneath this warm shower, I feel colder than when I was still out there in the rain.

# ELEVEN

## Eli

I walk into Amelia's bedroom and open the closet to take out a pair of jeans and a clean shirt. It's not a lot, but it'll have to do. The clothes reek of a vile barbarian I don't dare to call by name, but I'm glad he's dead.

Still, putting this on is better than running around completely soaked or worse … half-naked.

For a second there, I forgot about all the weight I carry on my shoulder and all the history that's marked on my back. Her kisses were divine, and her pussy tasted like heaven, and I wanted nothing more than to fuck her, so I did. I ravaged her and claimed her as I had always wanted to. Like we were star-crossed lovers meant to be.

I don't know if she truly wanted me or if she just let me. If she played the game to make me believe she wanted it just as badly. If so … she played it like a winner. And I loved every second of our twisted little game.

But pleasure comes with a downside, and that is the fall that comes after.

And my fall ... it was deep and harsh beyond imagination.

I stare at myself in the mirror, at the man I've become. Clothes that don't belong to me, a house that isn't mine, and a girl I've fallen head over heels for who will destroy everything I've worked so hard to keep.

Can I love her without losing myself? Without losing everything that makes me *me*?

What am I if not the house I grew up in and the rules that branded me?

These scars on my back belong there, along with all the sins that put them there, so then why am I so resentful about the pain they signify? Why do I refuse to let her see them?

\*\*\*

**Eleven Years Ago**

I've witnessed so many people suffer that I've become numb to it. But when my own father stands in front of the mirror as he flagellates himself with a whip, I still stop and stare, feeling my blood curdle at the sight of him.

Our eyes connect, but he doesn't stop, not even as fear settles in my bones and not even as the blood oozes down his skin and onto the carpet. He doesn't stop until the count of ten.

Ten strikes.

Ten for each of the punishments he applied to one of his sinners.

I swallow hard as he places the whip in a stand and grabs a towel from the chair, sliding it over his ragged back covered in scars. He's rarely shown himself without clothes on, especially not to me.

But then why did he call me over if he didn't want me to witness this?

I clutch the doorjamb as he comes toward me, his face still as stoic as ever. "It was time you learned the final lesson. Now you know."

I swallow as he passes me by, the sheer air of his presence making my knees buckle. Because that same pain he applied to himself … I've felt it before every time he struck me.

And that whip resting in that stand is merely an extension of his hands.

"It will be your turn soon," he whispers into my ear, and he pushes something into my hand.

I look down. It's a metal rod which he picked up from just beside the door that carries a mark. The mark of our house.

"This will be your tool," he says, the darkness in his voice making me shudder. "For every sin must be punished."

I helped him ... several times over these past few days. And now I must pay the price.

"These are the rules of our House," he says, his words weighing heavily on my soul. "Accept and do your duty."

I know it's my duty.

This is what I was born into, and whether I like it or not doesn't matter.

This is what I was supposed to do ... who I was supposed to become.

When he passes me, my fingers stiffen around the metal rod as I realize what this means. But a part of me still refuses to bend.

"Is that what you did to yourself after Mother died?"

He glances at me over his shoulder, pausing in his tracks. "I did what I had to do to keep this house from falling. You should do the same."

And as he walks off, my fingers clench the rod so hard that my nails dig into my skin until it cracks and bleeds.

\*\*\*

**Present**

I shake off the sudden unease clogging my brain and focus on getting back on track. I came here for a reason, with a purpose, and I must see it through to the end.

Amelia is right there with a towel slapped around her private parts when I march out the door. Her hands clutch the top while she crosses her knees, as though she feels the need to hide from me. And I wish she believed me when I told her that she didn't have to hide her body or her scars. No amount of sins could ever make me love her less.

But repeating it now would make me a hypocrite as I don't show myself to her either.

"What are we going to do?" she asks.

I frown and look away for a second, wondering how I'm going to say this.

"You're going to take me back there, aren't you?"

I refocus my attention on her. Of course she'd know instantly. She's too smart for her own good. "You have to come back."

"Why?" she asks, the hand with which she kept her towel in place forming a fist. "Give me one good reason."

Grinding my teeth, I stand my ground even when I want to wrap her in my arms so desperately. "Because I need you."

The look on her face briefly softens, and her grip loosens. She stares at me for a second, but that second feels like an infinite amount of time where not just my heart but my very soul is judged.

And here I was thinking I was the punisher, the one to make people confess. But my desires have revealed something hidden in plain sight. I am not the master of my own emotions. She is.

Her gaze on me, her thoughts and feelings about me, are all I care about. It gives her power over me. And that look on her face tells me she knows.

"I ... I ..." she stammers, shaking her head. "Please ..."

I narrow my eyes at her. "You know you have to come with me."

Her face tightens and shifts into something less sweet. "Even after everything we just did, after everything we talked about, you still want to do this?"

Her words hurt more than anyone else's ever could, and I force myself to ignore the pang in my stomach, along with my bleeding heart.

She must come. If I leave her here, there will be nothing left to save.

I hold out my hand. "Come back with me."

She frowns and swallows. "Do I even have a choice?"

I shake my head.

The silence between us is murderous, like a knife cutting straight into our souls. If nothing else will, the poisonous look on her face will kill me. But I have no choice. If she doesn't come ...

I look away. "There is a helicopter waiting for us."

"So what? If I don't come, you're just going to threaten me? Hurt me?"

I make a fist. I do not ever want to do the things she speaks of. If only she realized just how much I've grown to care for her.

"No wait, you'll just get your henchmen to do it for you," she scoffs, adding a tsk sound.

I turn around and walk into her room, grabbing the first

pair of women's pants and a shirt that I can find, and I throw them to her. She barely manages to catch them. "Put that on."

"Oh, not even a fancy dress?" she hisses.

I know she's trying to irk me, and I would be lying if I said it didn't get to me. It does. But what choice do I have? I'm not willing to give up this fight ... yet.

But she's pushing me to the brink. To the point where I'm not even sure why I continue or even bother. If only she knew the real choice I had to make ...

"No," she says, folding her arms.

I throw her a look. "Don't fight me on this."

"Or what? You're just gonna pretend all of this didn't happen?" She points at us both as if that will change my decision. "Why?"

"You will come with me, and you will rule the house with me."

Her eyes widen, but when she realizes I'm not backing away from that statement, her jaw drops. "You're serious?"

I nod.

"No," she retorts. "No, absolutely not."

I approach her, but she keeps backing away until we reach the wall. She holds up a flat hand to push me just far enough so I can't get near. "Stop."

"Or what? Are you scared of me now?" I ask, cocking my head. "You never were ... You just told yourself that so it would be easier to hate me. To say that I'm the enemy."

"You are," she hisses back, looking up at me with those

same doe-like eyes that always make my cock hard, even now.

I groan with frustration because I know I've had my share already, but it's never enough.

"Come, Amelia. Don't make this harder than it already is," I say, grabbing for her hand.

She tears away from my grip. "No. Give me a reason."

"Because I *need* you," I blurt out loud enough to shut her up. Or maybe, just maybe, it's because of the words I said.

It's quiet for some time, and I close my eyes and grumble to myself. I should not have said that. I really shouldn't have.

"Do you mean it?" she asks.

I sigh out loud and look away, unable to face my own emotions, let alone hers.

"Look at me when you tell me you want to take away my freedom just so you can have your way," she says through gritted teeth. "Look at me!"

For the first time, it's not me who's the master … it's her. She's the master of my strings and always has been from day one.

Her.

This has always been for her and because of her.

And I knew from the beginning all of this was going to be my undoing.

Yet I could never, ever stop.

A wretched smile forms on my face. "Yes."

Hatred fills her eyes, the look of which hurts far more than any of the scars on my back ever could.

"You can take my body. Destroy my soul. But my heart … that needs to be earned. And you have wasted your chance," she says, her voice riddled with agony and despair. "So take me. Take whatever's left of me. But know when you do that it was you—not my sin, or the loss of my loved ones—who destroyed me."

Her words are razor-sharp, sharper than any blade I've ever used to cut someone with. But the look in her eyes is as icy as never before. Like she flipped a switch and turned herself off. "I'll come on one condition." She swallows. "Let the other girls go."

I take in a deep breath. "You know I can't do that. They're not innocent."

"April is. Let her go," she says.

This is wearing me down. "I can't, and you know why. April's with us for a reason."

Her nostrils flare. "You can't even commit to this one request? Just one?"

I let out a long-drawn-out sigh and look away. "I'll see what I can do to … quicken the process."

She makes a face. "Fine."

I grab her hand before she changes her mind and makes this even more difficult. "Good. Then let's go."

When I turn around and walk, her immobility makes me stop. "Wait."

"You know this will make you a sinner too, right?" she

says. "Like you said, no one is without sin."

I frown before a wicked smile spreads on my lips, and I lean in, still holding her hand tight. "Exactly. I was born a sinner, and I'm going to die a sinner."

# TWELVE

## *Amelia*

With pain in my heart, I walk alongside him out of the apartment where I once felt at home. Now, it's nothing but a place filled with bad memories—memories of heartache, suffering, and death.

Maybe it's for the best. I wasn't going to get this apartment back anyway. I could never earn enough money to pay back the landlord for the missed rent, even though I was telling myself it was possible. It just wasn't meant to be.

I only hope that whatever I leave behind will remember me, and those memories will be better than the ones I have.

I sigh to myself as we step into the elevator.

Eli presses the button, and as the doors close, I realize it might be the last time I ever see that apartment. My eyes shut as I let out a breath while trying not to think about what's to come.

A sudden hand on my shoulder makes me jolt up and down.

"You don't have to worry," he says. "It's going to be okay."

I find that hard to believe.

A slight squeeze follows, making me hyper aware of his presence, of his body towering over mine right behind me.

"What are you thinking about?"

I flush, not daring to say it out loud.

Suddenly, his lips are near my ear. "Are you thinking about all the wickedly sinful things I'll do to you when we're back?"

I swallow. Hard.

I wasn't thinking about that at all. Only a little. Okay, maybe a lot. But I won't admit that, and I most certainly won't say that out loud. I might have gone with him, but he will never, ever claim my heart. I shut that option out entirely the second he took my free will away from me.

The doors open, and we step out. My eyes widen, and my jaw drops when someone presses the button to my doorbell outside the building. Jamie.

"No," I whisper.

*What is she doing here?*

Eli's arm wraps around my shoulder as he scurries me toward the door. Jamie's eyes land on me as Eli walks me to the door, my feet scraping against the floor, desperate to get away from this situation. But it's too late to go back and too late to stop her from seeing me. From seeing *us*.

The door opens. Eli takes me outside, his grip on my shoulder still as powerful as before. But I still manage to stop right as Jamie hovers next to us with her finger on my doorbell.

Her eyes widen too.

"Amelia?" she mutters.

Eli's grip tightens even more, and he leans over me to gaze straight into my eyes with a look that predicts thunder. My heart beats faster and faster.

"Hi … Jamie," I say.

She looks up at Eli, her pupils dilating. "You're the man from the library."

I frown and glance at Eli. So he was there, probably looking for me.

"What are you doing here?" I ask, trying to change the subject before she starts questioning him.

"I was looking for you," she says. "You were gone in the middle of the night, and I couldn't reach you anywhere."

Right. My phone. I completely forgot. Eli must have it.

"Are you back with Chris?"

I gasp in shock at the mention of his name.

"No, I—"

"He's gone," Eli fills in for me.

Jamie looks at him but doesn't say another word to him. "Are you okay?" She frowns, and then throws a look at Eli.

My lips part, but Eli's nails digging into my skin make

me stop. "I … I'm fine."

"You don't look fine," she says, gazing at him with full fervor. "Do I need to call someone?"

*The police? No. They'll try to search for Chris. And then I'll be put in jail. Oh God.*

"No, really, I'm fine," I say, lifting a hand.

She leans in. "Who is this guy?" she whispers.

"A friend," I say.

"A very … very … good friend," Eli adds, making me blush.

Jamie makes a face. "O-okay. Well, I just wanted to make sure you were okay. Seems you're still alive and well."

"You don't have to worry about me," I say, waving it off as if it's no big deal, even though I know where I'm going. I don't want her to worry. In fact, it would probably be better for her if she forgot I even existed. At least then, she'd be safe. Safe from all of this.

"All right, if you say so," she says, clutching her bag firmly against her. "I'll see you soon then?"

"I don't think so," I say, licking my lips. "I'm moving. Away from this city."

"Oh …" The look on her face darkens. "I thought you'd just come back, and now this."

"I know." I tuck my hair behind my ear.

It hurts to lie, but what other choice do I have? I don't want to cause a scene and risk Eli and his henchmen taking her too.

"I just changed my mind about living here. You know,

with all the memories and stuff. It just didn't feel right."

"Right …" she murmurs, looking away.

"But thank you," I sputter. "Thank you for all your help."

She smashes her lips together and nods. "Of course. Glad I could help."

Eli suddenly leans forward and squishes my shoulders with both hands now. "I'll take good care of her. We have to get going now."

"Bye!" I yell while taking one last look at her before I turn away with Eli's arm firmly around my shoulders. Only when I no longer see her do my eyes fill with tears, but I blink them away.

Eli brings me to a car on the other side of the street and opens the door for me, waiting until I get inside before he shuts the door. The silence that follows is bone-chilling. No more Jamie. No more library work. No more apartment. No more life. Everything is gone.

The door on the other side of the car opens, and Eli slides inside, shutting it behind him again.

"Thank you for not causing trouble," he says.

I look out the window at all the people bustling by, going about their regular lives like they deserve, blissfully unaware of the misery in mine.

A finger tips up my chin and forces me to look at him. "I mean it."

The tears can't stop forming in my eyes, no matter how much I try to keep them at bay.

He cocks his head. "Why are you crying?"

"I don't want her to get hurt," I say.

A gentle smile tugs at his lips. "Do you care that much? She was only a coworker."

"She helped me when no one else would," I answer.

His eyes narrow, and he stares at me for a moment. "You know ... your ability to trust and believe in people has me in awe."

My lips part, but before I can answer, he's already smashed his mouth onto mine, claiming a greedy kiss that makes my head spin. But I cannot let these delicious, heart-thumping kisses make me forget what he just took from me. Not once ... but twice.

So I force my heart to stay at bay, to let him have my body but not my love, and tears roll down my cheeks.

As his lips pull away from mine, he stares into my eyes and at my salty tears. With his thumb, he swipes them off, the look in his eyes solemn and full of turmoil.

"Did that do nothing for you?" he murmurs, his lips still so close to mine that I can taste them. "Is that woman all you really care about?"

But I ignore how good it felt. "I just want to keep her safe."

If that's the only good I have left to give this world, then so be it.

His eyes lower. "She will not be harmed."

He lets go of me and leans to the other side of the car, gazing out the window just like I was. But something tells me it isn't because he misses this world. It's because he misses the place where he could truly make me his.

And as he barks, "Go," at his driver, the world begins to unravel before me, along with my only shot at freedom.

But now I have something I didn't have before. Something I can use against him. *His heart.*

# THIRTEEN

## *Amelia*

The second I step foot back in that house, my heart feels like it's stopped beating entirely. House of Sin, the place where the unwanted and the criminals are sent when they have no more place in society. When their families and the ones they hurt demand a bigger punishment than jail. Suffering until there is true repentance … and I have certainly had mine.

I swallow hard as Tobias and Soren approach from the living room area, the looks on their faces thunderous.

"You made it back," Tobias tells Eli, and then he throws me a forsaken look. "With her."

Eli places a hand on my waist, a warm zing flooding my body, but I ignore it. I hate the way he makes me feel. "Safe and sound."

Tobias makes a face. "Well, at least one of our sinners is."

*Is he talking about Anna?*

"I think you swallowed too much salt water when you rescued yours," Eli quips.

Excuse me, have I just ended up in a sitcom or something? What is this? Why are they bantering like brothers about capturing people and taking them in as prisoners? Don't they understand what's wrong with that?

"I don't blame him for being salty," I say, rolling my eyes as they both stare at me as though they're surprised I could speak. But if anyone's allowed to be salty, it's me, and I'm more than willing to pile on top of it.

A definite smirk spreads on Soren's lips, and he looks away while Tobias throws him a deathly glare. "Really?"

Eli raises his brow at me. "Do you enjoy egging him on?"

"I enjoy egging all of you on." I fold my arms. "You dish out misery. You receive it."

Soren snorts out loud and then turns around and walks off toward that basement I'm not allowed to enter. Guess he wants no part in this. Tobias, however, doesn't seem at all amused. "You need to rein her in."

"No thanks," I reply.

Tobias's eyes narrow. "You seem to have gained quite the confidence since your escape. And I think it's time you were punished for it."

Eli steps in front of me. "The only one who will be touching her is me."

Oh my. I'd be lying if I said that didn't make the heat pool in my stomach.

"We already this conversation," Tobias said.

"And I think I made myself clear last time too," Eli replies.

I frown, and I grab Eli's arm to make him look at me. "What do you mean? What conversation?"

But instead of responding, he simply jerks himself free of my grip. "She is mine. End of story."

Tobias makes a face. "God ... I hope you're certain about this. I'd hate to see your choice go to waste."

*What choice?*

Eli's back muscles tighten hard as though he's holding a breath. "It won't. She's the one."

*The one? What?*

Tobias snorts and shakes his head. "Fine. You're going to destroy us, but whatever."

"I will make it work," Eli says.

"Of course, you will," Tobias scoffs, and he turns around, probably to walk off.

"We need this house to continue. You know that," Eli adds.

Tobias glances at us over his shoulder. "And you think she wants to be your wife?"

"Wife?!"

Both men now stare at me, and it's only then that I

realize I said that out loud. My cheeks turn crimson red from the sudden attention … and the fact that I'm to become his wife.

But I never agreed with that.

He never even asked.

And I don't know which one makes me more upset.

"No, no, no," I mutter, taking a step back. "I'm not marrying anyone."

Eli turns to me and grabs my wrist before I can walk away. "Stay."

I gulp at the seriousness in his voice and those dark eyes blazing with fire. Just one word, a simple command, is enough to make me listen. Why? Why does it come so easy to him? And why am I so happy to let him control me?

I'm so conflicted, and I hate it.

I hate that he made me feel things.

Because this man does not deserve any of my emotions. None.

He wasted that opportunity the minute he chose to bring me back here.

Tobias laughs. "I can't believe this. You've got to be kidding me. You didn't even tell her?"

Eli sucks in a breath. "*Tobias* … not now."

"You know what?" Tobias shrugs. "It's not my problem. You reap what you sow."

Then he saunters back upstairs to the other girls, I presume. Not that I care. I decided that the second I stepped into his car, I was going to shut myself off from everything they do.

But this ... how am I supposed to ignore this?

Eli ... wants me to become his wife?

No, not in a million years.

"I am *not* marrying you," I hiss, standing my ground.

Eli doesn't turn around. Doesn't even remotely acknowledge the fact that I rejected him on the spot, so I keep on talking, "Did you hear me?"

"I heard you," he says after a few seconds, turning all my hopes into dust that he'd ever care about my wishes.

I reach for his arm again, this time being a lot less civil about it. "What was Tobias talking about?"

"Nothing of importance," he says. "Now come."

When he tries to grab my hand, I pull away. "No. It was important. There's more going on than you've let on. Tell me."

His nostrils flare as he gazes at me from underneath those dark lashes, his eyes giving way to a certain kind of need that I haven't seen before. "This house needs to continue its legacy, like my father did before me and the owners of this house have done all the years before. And for that ..."

My eyes widen, and my jaw drops.

*No. He isn't talking about what I think he's talking about, right?*

"No ..." I murmur, my feet pushing me farther and farther away from him. "No, not in a million fucking years."

I can't spend another second in his vicinity.

All this time, I thought this was about my sins. His lust. My body.

And now that I find out it's about much more than that, I run upstairs, back to that hellish, godforsaken room that I spent so long trying to escape. Now I want nothing more than to be locked up here, far away from any of his schemes.

Because I'm not ready to be anyone's wife, let alone as a prisoner.

But even worse is the fact that he actually brought me back … just to give him a successor.

No child deserves to be born into this.

And I will die before I ever let him do that.

\*\*\*

# ELI

When she ran, I wanted nothing more than to chase her. But I knew that wasn't the right thing to do. She needs time to come to terms with what's been said and the truth beneath all that has happened to her.

I don't blame her for running off. I merely blame myself for keeping my true intentions hidden from her for far too long. I tell myself I had no choice, that I couldn't tell her sooner because of the implications. It would have killed her to know she had to spend an eternity in this house with me, so she'd never have gone with me freely.

But truthfully? I didn't want to tell her because I knew she would hate the idea … and that it would only drive her further away from me.

That is the sin I have to carry.

The pain is easy. But *this*? This is on another level entirely.

I sigh out loud and sink back into my comfy chair in my study, forcing myself to focus on the task at hand. Now that I'm finally home again, much needs to be done. Several more emails and calls have apparently come through from rich clients wishing to dump their family members on our doorsteps for some silly mistake. I'm not surprised, but we must draw a line between who is sincerely sorry and who is actually a sinner.

I cannot accept just anyone. They have to truly do something evil in order to end up here. Which I guess is why Amelia found it so hard to come to terms with the fact that many of these women are here out of their own free will. They know what they've done is terrible, and their only other options are jail … or death.

Being here, getting punished for their sins, is the easy way out.

Not for everyone, though. No, some would choose death over suffering. Many of them are men, most of whom we keep somewhere else, separate from the women. We don't take on a lot of them, as they usually end up dead instead of redeemed. Most of them deserve it too.

Not that I bother to care about any of the sinners. Not anyone ... except that one girl I happened to choose myself.

That one girl who caught my eye when I saw her out there on the streets, looking as perfect as I remember her being when I first saw her at my mother's funeral.

That one girl who was hiding behind a mountain of grief, punishing herself over and over, even though none of it was her fault. That girl who committed the most ungodly of crimes simply because she needed an escape.

And I realized then and there that we were not so different after all. In fact, I believe we were made for each other. If only she could see it.

I twist around a coin with my fingers that I've been using to distract me from the constant thoughts of Amelia swirling through my head. But it's obviously not working, so I clutch it hard and smack it on the table. Heads or tails ... the first will decide if I go.

And lo and behold ... of course, it's the head that shows.

A smirk forms on my face. Guess I'll go and face my demons, just as she has done to hers.

I march out of my study and head straight for her room. The room is unlocked, so no need to shove a key inside. Yet despite the freedom it's given her, she refuses to leave her room.

I open the door and pause. "Can I come in?"

It takes her a while to respond. "Why do you ask? It's your house."

"Because I respect your needs," I say.

Suddenly, the door is torn away from me. There she is, right in front of me, cocking her head at me with a certain clarity in her eyes that I can only describe as riveting.

"Really? *You*? Respecting *my* needs?" She snorts and shakes her head, then attempts to shut the door again, but my foot is already inside. "It means nothing to me."

She walks off and sits down on her bed with her arms crossed in a very defiant way that makes me want to grab her and fuck her senseless. I don't think she meant for that to happen, and I think she can see it in the way I look at her because she immediately puts her hands down on the bedding again, her skin flushing with heat.

"Stop," she says.

"Stop what?" I say as I enter the room and close the door behind me.

"Stop looking at me like that. Like I'm ... some kind of delicious snack."

I stand in front of her and tip up her chin with my index finger to make her look at me. "I cannot stop looking at you without losing myself ..."

Her eyes are full of melancholy and something else ... regret.

Regret she ever came with me?

Or regret she has feelings?

I swallow and sit down beside her on her bed. Her scooting away from me only confirms my worst thoughts.

"I don't want you to hate me," I say.

"Too late," she says.

Her words sting like a knife straight to the heart.

"Is there no part of you that can see past that?" I ask, looking into her eyes with full sincerity. "Could you ever love a man like me?"

"Love can't be taken. It can't be claimed. It can only be given," she says, and then she looks away, taking my heart along with her gaze.

I'm torn, but I made my decision, and I should stick with it. But then why can't I stop this horrible ache in my stomach?

I clear my throat and ignore the pang. "You will learn to love me again."

"You can wait until we're both beneath the ground," she hisses, and she pulls her feet up to her, clutching her legs as though it gives her comfort. But it's not the same kind of comfort I could give her.

My hand reaches for her hair, and I slide it aside, only to be swatted away.

"Fine," I say, and I get up, my nostrils flaring wide. "Then stay here for all I care."

"Fine," she retorts, and I march off.

But as I open the door, that same pain in my stomach punches me in the gut once more, and I find it hard to breathe, let alone leave.

I can't go like this. Not without saying something. Anything.

"I … I'm sorry," I mutter under my breath.

I don't think I've ever said those words before.

And I have no idea if they could ever encompass, let alone fix, all the things I've broken inside her. But it's a start.

Suddenly, she gets up from the bed and slams the door shut. I turn, and her finger is right up against my chest. "No!"

"No?" I raise a brow in confusion.

"No. You can't just say you're sorry. No. I won't accept it." She's never looked this upset.

"Then don't," I say, standing my ground. "But I still meant it."

She makes a face, her eyes glowing as though fire erupted inside them. She's grown so much fiercer ever since she found out about her own sin. As if she's finally realized she has more power than she thinks. And I'd be lying if I said it didn't turn me on.

"Sorry doesn't give me my freedom back," she says, shoving her finger into my chest. "All it does is make you a sinner."

"I know," I say, and I cover her hand with mine. "But being a sinner was always my fate."

She frowns and looks into my eyes, almost as if she's searching for something. "So you're going to keep me here forever?"

"If that's what it takes," I say, taking in a deep breath.

"I am *not* going to be your wife," she says, ripping her hand out of my grasp. "End of story. This piece of ass is off the market." She points at her behind as though it's something I haven't already savored. But I do agree that I'd be very upset if I couldn't have another bite.

"Now leave," she barks, folding her arms. "Unless you're telling me you're going to take *that* freedom from me too."

I reach for her, and she flinches the minute I touch her chin. It's not a flinch from fear, but a flinch of a woman desperate to tell herself she doesn't want me the same way I want her. But this attraction between us is undeniable, no matter how many times she tries to deny both herself and me.

"No … I could never." I caress her cheeks briefly. "But I cannot bear the thought of being without you either."

"Then I'm going to stay here and rot away," she says through gritted teeth.

Before I can reply, she marches off to the windows, wistfully staring outside as though she misses it already.

Maybe I really am the monster she thinks I am. I've taken away her freedom … but at what price?

There is nothing more to be uncovered and no more sins to be punished for. What then do I have left to bargain with? Nothing.

And she must know this.

So I sigh and open the door, determined not to come back until I have something, *anything* to convince her to stay by my side.

Because I don't *just* need her to be my wife or to make an heir.

"I need you … to live," I say, and then I close the door behind me.

# FOURTEEN

## Amelia

When he said he was sorry, I almost believed him. Almost.

He'd never said those words before ... and they made me hungry, so hungry for more.

But then I remembered that it is all I have left to bargain with. Not my body; he's already had that. No, all that's left is forgiveness ... which I refuse to grant him.

I'll die on this hill if I have to. I have nothing else, so why bother?

But what did he mean by "I need you to live"? I am very much alive, so I don't understand why he'd say such a thing. Unless he means that I'm in danger. Maybe that's why he dragged me back here.

Or maybe ... he means something else entirely, and I don't understand shit.

I sigh to myself as I stare out the window at the beautiful trees in the distance, those same trees I once ran through just to escape his grasp. And look at me now, back where I started, right back in his clutches. And I didn't even put up a fight. I just let him drag me back to his car like it was supposed to happen.

After a few hours have passed, I've had enough of this. Grumbling to myself, I get up from my seat and go to the bathroom, where I draw a scorching hot bath for myself. If I can't have my freedom, at least I can enjoy all the luxurious things this house has to offer, like this super creamy and expensive-looking soap that I lather all over myself. Maybe I'll have an expensive wine tonight, and I'll order them to give me the entire bottle.

What is Eli going to do? Say no?

He can't. If he did, I'd only have more reason to hate him, which is the last thing he wants.

No, he wants me to adore him. Like I did when he made me remember what I did and hugged me through it all, when he came to my rescue in my own apartment and kissed all the worries away, and when we talked and talked until we could no more and stood under that warm shower, fucking the pain away.

My thighs clamp together as I think about it, my pussy forgetting that it should no longer clench for him. But I force myself to erase him from my mind.

Until he suddenly steps into my bathroom.

I shriek. "Jesus."

One look at him, and I'm already completely overcome with lust as he stands there in his navy blue suit like some kind of perfect gentleman. "Apologies. I didn't mean to scare you."

I force myself to look away. "I'm not afraid of you."

"I know," he says with such certainty that it catches me off guard. "If you're not too busy …"

*Busy? Me?*

I snort at the thought.

"I'd like to take you somewhere tonight," he says.

I frown and gaze at him over my shoulder. "Where?"

There's a slight smile on his face, and I'm not sure if it's a trap or not. "It's a surprise."

Definitely a trap.

"Not interested." I continue lathering myself with soap.

"I think you are," he says. "I'm quite sure you'll like this."

I sigh and then stand in the bath, putting my naked body on full display. It doesn't faze me, but the longing gaze in his eyes makes him do a double take, and that … that does make me grin on the inside. But I won't show that to him.

"Ah … I'll wait outside," he says, and his head quickly disappears.

A smirk forms on my face. I get out and dry myself off before wrapping the towel around my body and marching outside. He's right there, reading one of the many books from the shelves of the old bookcase in this room.

The second he notices me, the book snaps shut. His eyes swath over my body as if he's taking it all in, and it makes me feel as if his hands are already on my bare skin. Goddammit. Will I ever get rid of this obnoxious feeling? I guess not.

But I would rather die than admit that to him, so I stay quiet and stare at him, arms crossed.

He puts the book down, never breaking eye contact. "Have you read these?"

"All of them," I respond.

A gentle smile tugs at his lips. "I'll see to it that you get some new ones."

"Fantastic," I reply.

He cocks his head. "Do you have to be so cold?"

"Do you have to be so evil?"

He rolls his eyes and sighs out loud. "Touché."

I walk to my closet and grab the most ludicrous dress by Chanel I can find. He doesn't stop looking at me, though, not even as I throw the towel off and start to dress, taking ample time to show him every inch of my skin that I'll never let him touch again.

"Are you so intent on making me suffer, Amelia?" he asks.

"As much as possible," I retort, swiftly turning around.

His stance shifts. "I have someone you need to see." He's immediately changed the conversation, but I'm not sure I mind.

"Who?" I put on the rest of my clothes and step into my pumps.

He holds out his arm, waiting for me to hook mine through it. "Let me show you."

I roll my eyes. "This had better be worth it."

"Trust me when I say, you'll love this," he says as he takes me out of the room.

"This had better not be some surprise marriage because I will shove that ring up where no one will ever be able to find it," I say, which makes him laugh.

"No, contrary to what you may think of me, I don't enjoy fueling your already seething hatred for me."

I wouldn't put it past him to trick me into one, that's for sure.

"C'mon," he says as we walk up the stairs. "It's this way." I've never been to this floor, and gazing down makes me dizzy. The paintings on the ceiling are even more beautiful this up close.

"Who made those?" I ask out of the blue, momentarily forgetting he's not just some random guy.

He looks up at the ceiling, too, marveling at its beauty. "A famous painter. Danton Angelo."

I snort. "Really? That's his name?"

"Yes. His parents probably thought it was funny," he replies. "Guess they didn't expect him to actually become a painter."

Impressive. But even more impressive is the fact that Eli could pay for this.

"So you earn that much from punishing women, huh?" I mutter.

"Not just women. Men too." His eyes break contact with the painting and settle on me again. "People are willing to pay the price for such an arrangement."

"I should be amazed, but I'm not," I say, sighing. "People are evil."

"Or they are just looking for alternative routes," he says, a smirk forming on his face. "C'mon."

He pulls me along with him to the right side of the banister, where there are rooms as well.

"What's on this floor?" I ask. "I've never been here before."

"Because it was forbidden," he replies, making me gulp. "Relax." He laughs. "I make the rules. I decide when something is forbidden or not."

I suck in a breath and look away. "I don't care."

"Of course you don't." Why do I get the sense he doesn't at all believe me?

"But if you must know … This is Tobias's quarters."

My eyes widen. "The entire floor?"

"Just this side," he muses. "The other one is for Soren, but he prefers to remain downstairs for some reason." He shrugs.

He knocks on a door at the end of the walkway, and we wait.

"Yes?"

My pupils dilate at the sound of that voice.

*It ... it can't be.*

Eli pushes the door open.

On the bed is Anna ... a book in her hands, rosy, pink skin, no more tubes or beeping machine. And a happy smile on her face the moment she looks up and sees it's me.

She survived.

And not just that ... she looks like she's thriving.

Tears well up in my eyes. "Anna ..."

She puts the book down on the bed and sits on the edge. "Hey."

I just stand there awkwardly, not knowing what to do or what to say. But I'm glad, so glad that she's actually here. That she's alive and well, for as far as I can tell.

The last time she saw me, she was running for her life, trying to escape. But I didn't know back then that she was on the verge of her own ruin and wanted to go beyond what I would ever consider. And I have no clue what to do or say to her.

I swallow back the nerves. "How are you feeling?"

She smiles. "Okay. My muscles still ache, and I feel like I've been hit by a bus. But other than that ... okay. Which is more than enough, considering the circumstances." She laughs a little, and so do I, even though they both sound horribly uncomfortable.

"I'll let you two have your moment," Eli suddenly says, leaving the room.

"I'm glad you're okay," I tell Anna, stepping closer. "The last time I saw you, you were—"

I can't even say it out loud without choking up.

She looks down at the bed, clutching her hands. "I know." She sighs out loud. "I know what I've done."

I approach her and sit down beside her on the bed. It's quiet for some time, and I don't know what to say to make this all okay. So I grab her hand instead and squeeze it gently, hoping that she understands what I mean.

"You have nothing to apologize for," I say. "I didn't know what you were going through."

Tears well up in my eyes. "But I am sorry. I put you through so much pain."

I silence her with a big hug. "Don't. I'm the one who should be apologizing. I pushed you to run. I should've stopped to ask you what you wanted, what you really needed."

She cries in my arms for a while, and I stay with her, hoping that I provide at least a little bit of comfort by being there.

"Thank you," she whispers after a while.

"For what?"

"For being here. For talking to me. For trying. For staying by my bedside, even when I wasn't there."

I lean back and brush away her tears. "Of course. Where else was I going to go?"

She pulls back and tucks her hair behind her ear. "I thought ... you were mad at me."

I shake my head. "No, I'm just ..." I sigh and look away for a second. "I wish I had known before we ran."

"You mean ... what I did?" She gulps, her cheeks turning crimson. "I wasn't allowed to speak to anyone about it because of the dangers, and I desperately don't want to end up in jail." She rolls her eyes while simultaneously opening them wide. But then she sighs out loud and looks away again. "But I'm sorry I lied to you."

"I understand," I say.

"So one of the guys told you?" she asks. When I nod, she starts twiddling her fingers. "I ... my parents ... I didn't want them ..." Tears well up in her eyes, and I quickly hug her tight.

"Shh ... you don't have to tell me."

I'm not just doing this because it's hard for her to talk about. I'm also doing it for me. Because I'm that girl who didn't have parents, who lost them when she was too young to be an orphan.

And she's the girl who wished them away.

It's hard to empathize with that, but at the same time, I know there must be a reason for her to hate them so much, and it's not my job to judge.

"What happens now?" I ask.

She smiles. "I don't know. Tobias wants to keep me at the house in case I relapse."

I look her directly in the eyes. "Is he good to you?"

She nods a couple of times. "Better than I deserve." Her entire face flushes, and she attempts to hide it behind her hair, but I still notice.

I was so worried about her, yet when I look at her now,

I only see a woman who's survived the worst and lives to better her life. Someone who truly wants to repair the broken parts in her. But what's driving her? It couldn't be …

Tobias?

Could it be?

"Is this your room now?" I ask.

"Tobias wants me to stay here with him," she says, a soft but quirky smile settling on her face. "So he can keep an eye on me."

"Hmm …" I don't know how to respond.

She gawks at me. "What?"

"Nothing." I raise my brows and look away. "I was just thinking about how he treated you, and—"

"He treats me fine," she interjects. "More than fine."

"Right." I smile. "Well, I'm glad."

"Is Eli not treating you right?" she suddenly asks.

The question is so abrupt, so invasive, that I turn entirely silent, but my lips still part as though they have something to say. He did treat me fine … until I found out he was going to bring me back here when he knows I will never be happy with losing my freedom.

But isn't it the same for her? She's being kept here even after confessing her sins. What else could there be except for the mad cravings of men?

Doesn't she hate him for it?

"Are you okay with Tobias keeping you here?" I ask.

"Yeah, why wouldn't I be?"

She makes it sound so normal. Like it was meant to be this way, but it's not.

"You committed a sin, okay? Your grandparents decide not to have you prosecuted the regular way but send you here, fine. But you confessed. You were done. Why are you still here? You're supposed to be free."

She looks up at me with a certain melancholy in her eyes that reminds me of a forlorn woman waiting by the ocean for her longlost sailor lover.

"I ... I ... I don't know," she says, her cheeks turning strawberry red again.

I take her hand. "Is he keeping you here as a prisoner?"

"No!" She stands up, releasing herself from my grip. "No, it's not like that."

"But he's one of *them*," I say.

"Is that what you are to Eli?" she asks, raising a brow. "A prisoner?"

When I nod, she sighs and starts pacing around the room. "I'm sorry. It's just that ... that's not at all what Tobias is like. Sure, he might be arrogant. And he's definitely dominant ..." Her face flushes with heat again. "But he's also kind and gentle with me."

She stops in her tracks and bends over to squish her stomach, and I immediately get up and support her before she falls over. "Careful."

"Sorry ... I forget how weak I still am," she mutters as I help her sit back down on the bed.

"I get it," I say.

"I hate what I did. All of it. The second I did it, I regretted it," she says. "And I hate that I can't ever take it back."

We sit there for a while, not saying anything, but no words sometimes say more than any ever could.

"But more importantly, I hate how much I hurt him."

*Him? She can't be talking about Tobias?*

Has he twisted her mind so far, or has she truly fallen for him?

I swallow hard, considering my own fate and how I too have kissed Eli, willingly … and let him fuck me, willingly. Who am I to judge her choices if I made the same ones?

"I get it," I say.

"Do you, though?" She raises a brow at me. "I mean, you don't look madly in love to me."

I snort and hide a blush behind my hand. "Well, no, not like that."

"But in some other way, you do like him?"

"*Liked*," I correct. "And it was only in a moment of stupidity."

She chuckles, and so do I, and eventually, she ends up with her head against my shoulders. We sigh in sync. "We're fucked, aren't we?" I murmur.

She nods against me. "That's what you get for sinning hard. The sins only come back to bite you in the ass."

# FIFTEEN

*Amelia*

I knock twice before entering his office. Eli's nowhere to be seen, so I walk around and wait for him to arrive. His bedroom door is shut, but maybe he locked it on purpose because he doesn't want uninvited guests. And right now, I'm not sure where exactly I stand.

I stroll around and touch the books on the bookcase, finding a curious mix of psychology alongside handwritten ones. I pull one out and flip through the pages, all of them filled with dates and names, along with specific punishments applied. Yikes.

I swiftly put the book back and grab another one, sifting through it. Every page is filled with handwritten text about rules and judgments about what to do in certain situations, such as when the sin is completed and the suffering of the one who did the punishing. The word death somewhere on the page makes all the hairs on the back of my neck stand.

This looks like an heirloom. Is this handed down from generation to generation? When I get to the last few pages, I have my answer. Eli's handwriting is right there, along with all his punishments, and my name and sin. And on the last page is a symbol marked in blood.

"Doing some light reading, I see."

His voice makes me spin on my heels, but it's his form that makes me drop the book entirely. And by form, I mean well-shaped body like an Adonis standing naked right in front of me.

My eyes widen, saliva building in my mouth while my gaze roams over his aptly sculpted torso, the rugged abs underneath, and that V-line that leads to an oh, so delicious…

*No, I can't think about that. Stop it, Amelia.*

"Cat got your tongue?" he muses, his brow rising flirtatiously.

I avert my eyes and put a hand in front of my eyes. "My God …"

"God is kind of busy right now," he says, stepping toward me. "But I'm here if you need something."

I roll my eyes but force myself to look the other way. Too bad my hand has fingers, and they can't help split apart to catch a glimpse of that handsome body and that *oh my God, did I really have that inside me* thing.

He grabs a black turtleneck draped over his chair and throws it on, which is a curious thing to do if you ask me when you don't even have underwear on. But I don't think that's a coincidence. In fact, I'm more inclined to believe he's giving me a piece of my own medicine.

"It's not forbidden to look, you know," he says with a smug smile on his face. "You've done it plenty of times before."

Now I really can't stop the redness from overtaking my face.

"Principles," I mutter. "And would you please put something on?"

He suddenly grabs my hand and lowers it. I hadn't realized he was already this close to me. "Now why would I do that?"

"Because it's cold," I hiss. I don't care if it's cold. I just know that I'm getting way too hot, and that needs to stop.

"Oh, I'm not cold … far from it, in fact," he jokes, but the rolling sound his voice makes at the end pushes all my buttons. "I think it's because you can't stop looking."

The dirty, full-on smirk that follows makes me want to slap it off his face.

"Fine, then stay naked for all I care," I retort, and I swiftly walk to the other side of his desk just to get out of the precarious situation I was definitely drifting toward.

I reach for a photograph standing on the edge of the desk. There's a middle-aged woman on it, and the somber look on her face captures my attention. Something about her eyes is so familiar, but I can't put my finger on it.

"Why did you come to my study?"

A soft squeal leaves my mouth as I spin on my heels again. He's right behind me, still wearing only that dammed turtleneck, but thankfully, he's added some briefs to the mix. Phew. "If not to stare at my body."

I put down the photograph and fold my arms to create some much-needed distance and remind myself he isn't as delicious as my mind makes him out to be. "I just came to say thank you for letting me see Anna."

He tilts his head. "You're welcome."

I frown, cocking my head. "Okay."

"What?" He raises his brow.

"Well, you don't have to be all cocky about it," I scoff.

He shrugs. "You thanked me. And I like seeing you grateful." There's that insufferable smirk again, the one that continues to make my heart gallop, especially when he runs his fingers through his dripping wet hair. But dammit, I promised myself I wouldn't go there again. He stole my freedom, and with it, he stole my dreams at a happy ever after. I won't let him claim my heart and my life along with it. He wants to keep me here? Fine, but I'll be heartless like a stone-cold bitch.

"I take it back," I say, and I turn away from him.

"Aw, c'mon," he mutters, putting a hand on my arm.

I push him off. "No. I think you only did that to make me like you again. It's not going to work."

His brows rise. "You see right through me, don't you?"

Not sure if he means that in a serious or a sarcastic, you're being a bitch way. Not that it matters, because I'll take anything over seeing that smug face of his again when he notices I'm having trouble fighting the attraction.

Suddenly, he grabs my wrist and holds on to it. "Lucky for you, I see right through you too."

"Lies," I say.

But he corners me against the desk, pinning my wrist and me along with it. "I think you know I'm not the one lying here," he muses, his lips twisted, like a devil trying to persuade me to step into the fire with him. Every inch he leans in, it becomes harder to resist temptation. "And I think you know as well as I do that you want me."

I try to ignore the growing hunger pooling in my body. I must always remember who he is and what he does for a living. "Is this what you do? Is that how you get them to stay?"

He frowns. "What are you talking about?"

"The others," I hiss. "Don't play coy with me. I wasn't the first girl you had in this house."

He cocks his head and snorts. "Oh, you mean previous sinners."

I gulp as the thoughts swirl through my head about all the filthy things he's done to my body and just how much I enjoyed them.

"I have fucked some of my guests previously," he says. "But none since you came into my life." With the back of his hand, he strokes my cheek. "But that isn't really what you're asking now, is it? You want to know if we're exclusive. Because you're jealous."

My eyes widen, and my jaw drops. "I am *not!*"

That infuriating smirk reappears on his face, and I'm about this close to just smacking him. "You don't have to fight over me, Angel. I'm all yours. Have been for a long time."

"Stop," I hiss, trying to shoo the blush from my cheeks. "This is not about that."

"Then what is it about, hmm?" he muses, that same insufferable smirk still lodged firmly on his face. "Because it seems to me like it is."

He's so close now that I can feel his breath on my lips, and my eyes instinctively close. "Remember when we were under the shower at your place? How desperate you were for more kisses?" he whispers. "How desperate you were for me to fuck you?"

I gasp when our lips touch, and my breath hitches in my throat. How does he so easily subdue me? Does he know so well how to dominate me, with all those thick muscles and those dirty smiles? Or is it because I succumb so easily to a man who offers me just a whiff of an escape?

"Let me love you, Amelia," he whispers, his words tugging at my heartstrings.

And within seconds, his mouth lands on mine.

At first, his kiss is soft as his lips swipe gently across mine. Like he intends to show me he can be sweet, and that he wants to take this slow to get me used to the idea. He never kissed me like this before, so full of emotion, as though he wants nothing more than for me to love him back.

But I can't. I can't love someone who does this to people. To me.

"I can't," I whisper, but it's futile against his lips. "I can't give up my freedom."

His hands find their way up my arms until he cups my face with both hands, desperate for more kisses.

"And I can't give you up," he says between kissing me.

His tongue swivels between my lips until they part, and he claims my mouth too. I can't stop this onslaught of polarizing emotions swirling through me. I hate him. I hate him so much for what he's done to me, yet at the same time, I can't even say no, can't push back and deny him because my own body wants him just as badly as he wants me. Lust is threatening to overtake me, but I don't know if I really want to stop it.

And soon, his hands find their way down my neck to my back, where he fumbles with the zipper. With a grunt, he tears the dress down, setting my body on fire, while never taking his lips off mine.

"Let me take you," he groans against my lips. "I want you all for myself. I need you, Amelia."

I'm torn between hate and lust, between never wanting to see him again and wishinghe would kiss me and fuck me until I forget who we truly are and stop thinking about the fact he's the one who stole my freedom away.

And I can't fucking stop.

Can't stop letting him touch me, his hands grasping my boobs, his mouth moving down to suck on my nipples until they're taut. And dammit, if it wasn't the best feeling in the world.

I thought my torment was going to stop once I found out what I did. All this time, I worked so hard toward getting to know my own secrets, and now that I finally do … nothing's changed. I'm still in his clutches, still desperate for him to take me.

Why didn't it end when it should have?

"I thought this was supposed to stop when the sinner had confessed?" I say through heated breaths.

"It doesn't have to," he whispers against my skin. "It can go on forever … and ever … and ever." His tongue dips out to lick me, circling my nipple before he comes back up to claim my mouth again.

And boy, does he claim it. It's like he wants to lay waste to me. Conquer me and leave nothing behind. Not even scraps. As though he's afraid that if he doesn't take all I have to give, someone else will.

And I yield to his powerful gaze, his all-consuming kiss, even when I told myself I never would again.

"Oh, Angel, you undo me," he murmurs.

But I'm no angel. I'm a liar and a sinner. Just like him.

So maybe he's right after all …

Maybe we do deserve each other.

***

# ELI

Finally, I have my angel in my arms again.

I knew she would come to me eventually. It was only a matter of time before she succumbed and let me in again. And I waited patiently for the moment to arrive.

But I'll save the arrogant smirks for later. Right now, I want nothing more than to bury my face between these tits and fuck her until she screams my name.

No amount of kisses will ever be enough when it comes to her. I must have her in every way, shape, and form.

All this time spent apart has been too much for both my heart and my body to take, and I want nothing more than for her to surrender to me.

Be mine, not just the body but the soul too.

And as I plant kisses all over her body, I can feel the barrier between me and her break. Slowly but surely, she's opening up to the idea of being with me, and it exhilarates me to no end.

My tongue swipes over the roof of her mouth, and a groan follows. I can't stop myself when every inch of her body begs to be taken. I grasp her waist with both hands and lift her up from the floor, swiping aside everything that was on my desk before I set her down.

Screw the consequences because any mess can be

cleaned up later. Before she protests, I fiercely fist her hair and cover her mouth with mine, leaving no second wasted.

Her hands rest on my chest, my pecs tightening in response to her every touch. I'd be lying if I said she didn't have an effect on me. She has more than any other woman before and more than I'd ever let on.

No one has gotten this close to me before, this close to unraveling my heart. But she has. She's twisted me in ways even I didn't see coming from miles ahead.

When I found her, after years of searching and searching, I thought I would be content with watching her, waiting until she sinned so I could take her into the house to fuck her until she'd confess, and that everything would be over then.

But I was wrong. It was far from over. It was only the beginning of our tumultuous affair. Every time I kissed her, I grew closer to the only truth that ever existed. I didn't just want to punish her for her sins. I wanted her to be mine forever.

So I take and I take, planting greedy kisses all over her body, groaning with delight at the idea that I get to do this every single day. Fuck the others, and fuck the consequences. I don't even care about the house anymore. If I can have her, I'm more than happy.

I kiss her hard and fast, not giving a shit in the world about what it means or how addicted I've become to the taste of her lips, to the feel of her tongue wrapping around mine, to the scorching heat between our bodies as we collide.

With my palm, I shove her down onto the desk and grasp her dress, tugging it down and off until her bare pussy is exposed. No more panties; she's learned that much since she came here. And I enjoy nothing as much as the sight of this pussy right here.

I grasp her waist and tear down my underwear before spreading her legs and thrusting into her. Her mouth forms an o-shape, a moan escaping right before I smash my lips onto hers. My body is on hers as I bury myself deep inside her, her pussy clutching firmly around my cock. She shivers underneath me but still wraps her legs around me.

I smile against her lips. "I love the way you feel against me … how you yield so easily from my touch."

"No …" she whispers. "I hate it."

"Don't hate … love it the way I do," I reply, pressing another kiss against her needy lips, which pucker up just for me.

With every thrust, her body buckles and her breath falters. We're fucking like animals in heat, the desk scooting across the floor with each of my pumps.

I don't even care that we've made a mess. All I want is to claim her and prove to her that we can't resist each other.

We belong together, body and soul, and it's about time she realized that.

I thrust in hard and fast, not giving a shit if someone might come in or not.

"Fuck …" she whispers, "Stop."

My brow rises as I pause, still inside her. "You sure?"

"No," she hisses, wriggling underneath me like some coy little lamb desperate to get closer to the lion. "Don't stop."

I laugh. "You sure can't make up your mind, can you?" I plunge in once more until she moans out loud. "Keep moaning, Angel. Those tell me the truth."

"Fuck," she says through gritted teeth. I thrust in again. "You."

A smirk spreads on my lips, and I grasp her wrists and pin them to the desk. "This is what you get for coming into my room."

She may hate me, but she doesn't hate the way I make her feel. And I'd be lying if I said it wasn't the same for me.

My cock grows harder inside her, her wet juices filling me with lust to the point of turning into a beast. I'm so close to the edge that I can almost taste it.

Suddenly, her eyes burst open, and she shoves her feet against my thighs until I step back, forcing my dick out of her. She expertly slides off the desk and wraps her lips around my cock, taking me in so deep that it makes me groan.

This isn't what I had planned.

But it's too late to go back.

The sensations are too much. I come inside her throat, filling her up to the brim while buried deep inside.

She gulps it all down with glee, her fingers fluttering across her clit until she too starts to moan, and I know the sound all too well.

She just came by her own doing, but it wasn't my cock inside her that made her fall apart. Nor was it my cum that she so desperately swallowed down.

I pull out and stare down at her, clutching the desk for support as my knees feel heavy. She swipes her hand across her lips to rid herself of any leftovers, her eyes boring straight into mine.

The corners of my mouth go down while hers go up, her eyes sparkling with pleasure. But it's not the kind of pleasure one gets from sex. It's the kind of pleasure that only comes from power.

And I hate it.

She used me.

"You did that on purpose, didn't you?" I growl, my dick getting flaccid already, even though I was planning on giving her so much more.

She cocks her head, her devious little plan coming to light in the form of a smile. "I told you … I am not ever going to bring a child into this."

My nostrils flare at the thought of her denying me this.

I know it's wrong, and I know that it should be a decision we make together, but this? Stooping this low, trying to fuck me, to persuade me to give in, only to turn on me at the very last second just so she can get away with fucking me without giving me everything I want? That's low.

Lower than I expected her to go.

She gets up from the floor, pulling up her dress and

zipping it up again right in front of me. "Should have thought about that before you tried to have sex with me," she muses. "What are you going to do? Punish me for it?"

"You know this will not change anything, right?" I growl, angered that she would pull this stunt with me.

I should bend her over my desk and spank her right here and now.

But if I did that, I would only be proving her point.

She knows exactly what she did, and she did it anyway because I have nothing to hold against her anymore. No sins left unpunished, nothing to yield over, nothing that I can use to make her submit. And by adding marriage and a child to the mix, I just sealed my own fate.

She will never grant me the most delicious parts of her body again.

Just to take power back from me.

"Bye, Eli," she says as she walks past me with her head held high.

I stand there, still panting like a crazed beast, wishing I could ravage her any way I want.

If I take it from her ... I will be no better than the man she hated so much that she killed him for it.

My fist balls.

No, I will wait, and wait ... and wait ... for however long it may take for her to come to her senses. For her to realize that she does, in fact, need me, want me ... love me.

Just as I love her.

And I will make her understand.

Make her forgive me.

No matter the cost.

And as I gaze at the fire in which the hot iron already lies await, I know what I must do now.

# SIXTEEN

*Amelia*

**A few days later**

On the living room couch, I leisurely lounge while sipping the coffee I got from one of the staff members. Apparently, they know now not to get in my way because there is a price to pay, and it isn't just my anger that will hurt them. My happiness doesn't only benefit me anymore. Eli wants a piece of the pie as well.

After our rendezvous in his office, I clearly got my point across. I had expected Eli to follow me, berate me, take me back into his room, and fuck me until I begged him. Instead, he let me walk out the door like it was nobody's business.

To say I was surprised was an understatement,

considering our history.

But maybe he really did change after all.

Maybe he does care.

Which means I can use this situation to my advantage and get all the privilege one could receive in a place like this. All I need to do now is give the same kind of freedom to the other ladies, which is exactly what I'm planning on doing once Eli finally musters up the courage to come and find me.

I haven't seen him for a while now, and I wonder if he's busy with work, or if he's trying to seduce others to confess their sin to him. The mere thought makes me crinkle up some of the paper in this book I was reading.

I shouldn't let myself get carried away by my emotions, but it's hard when you let your heart join the game once before. Back when I was in my apartment, and Eli practically bared his soul to me, almost confessing his love on the spot.

It uncoiled the bonds I'd secured around my heart, and it made me fall for him. Made me wish I could kiss the pain away, made me forget all the things he did to me, made me … want him.

I wanted him. More than anything.

When we fucked under the shower, all I wanted was for him to stay, forget everything that happened between us, and focus on the here and now … because I knew we had no future.

There is no "we" when he and I are from two different worlds.

When he only wants to keep the bird locked in its cage, it will always find a way to escape.

And I would rather die brandished a liar for not being truthful about my feelings to him than as someone who betrays her own soul. No matter how good the sex felt, under the shower, on his desk ... anywhere and everywhere. There is nothing else I have left to give. Nothing else ... but my soul, and I refuse to offer it up.

I release the page from my grip and unfurl it, attempting as well as I can to flatten it, but I know it's no use. Once crumpled, a paper can never become pristine again.

And for some odd reason, that reminds me of me.

Suddenly, someone knocks on the door, and my ears perk up.

I put the book on the table. "Yes?"

When Eli steps inside, I take a big gulp of my coffee and swallow it down. I'd rather let the heat burn my throat than let him rake me up in a tainting stare.

"Hello, Amelia," he says, his voice commanding but respectful.

I put down the cup. "Do you need something?"

He raises his brow and continues to stare at me while the clock ticks away behind me on the wall, but I am not going to give in. "Not even a hi?" he says, adjusting his navy blue blazer so that it covers his mighty abs that protrude through the white shirt.

I just raise a brow back at him, trying to ignore the fact that he looks handsome in this outfit.

A smirk forms on his lips as he shakes his head. "Guess I deserve that much."

"Yes. Yes, you do," I quip, unable to stop myself.

His tongue darts out to wet his lips, and I tell myself I'm not looking. I'm definitely not looking.

"Can we talk?" he asks, stepping forward.

I lean back on the couch and pull my knees up to lie down, leaning my head on my wrist. "Talk."

Mostly because I do not want him to sit down next to me.

He looks around and decides to sit down on the fauteuil on the opposite side of the table. It's silent for a few seconds while he looks around, and I do the same, trying desperately not to look at him for fear that I may do something I despise. Like ... getting on top to kiss him and let him fuck the pain away.

But I can't. I cannot go there. Not with what's at stake.

"You've been reading," he says, and he looks at the stack beside my cup of coffee. "A lot."

"Just wasting time," I scoff.

"Time you could be spending with me," he retorts, leaning forward on his elbow too, his biceps thickening from the pressure. And I'm stuck wondering why I even noticed.

"Tsk ... As if." I roll my eyes and pick up my coffee again and take another sip.

"Is the prospect of being with me so unreasonable to you?" he asks with a serious tone, which captures me off guard.

"I …" I swallow down the coffee and put the cup down with great intention, then look up at him from underneath my lashes. "You promised me that it would be over once I'd confessed. That I would be free."

His nostrils flare as he sucks in a breath, still intent on listening to every single one of my words.

"You lied. You betrayed me. You don't even live by your own rules."

"You fled the premise and tried to involve others," he rebukes. "As far as I can tell, we both broke the rules."

"I didn't make them!" I yelp. "And I never told you I would follow them. I was never asked. The other girls all came willingly, but you stole me like it was your God-given right."

His body grows rigid in the seat as though he finally realizes the gravity of the situation.

"I will never, ever—"

"Stop," he interrupts, tilting his head backward.

I sigh and look away. I knew it. Of course, he never wants me to finish that sentence. Because doing so would mean finally saying the one thing I've wanted to scream at him since the day he took me.

"You're right. I took you. Not just because of your sin," he admits. "But because I wanted you. I wasn't ready to admit that at the time, but I am now."

"That doesn't change anything," I say. "All you did was deceive."

"And I apologize for that," he says.

I narrow my eyes at him. He really thinks I'm ready to forgive him like it's easy?

"It's not going to be that easy."

"Then tell me what I can do," he asks, the most sincere look on his face.

I raise my brow at him, but he just does not let up. So I sigh. "The least you could do is respect my wishes."

"Which are?"

"I want to be left alone," I respond, looking him dead in the eyes.

A tepid smile appears on his face. "You know I can't do that."

I sigh out loud and get up. "Well, then you're just going to have to deal with a snarky me." I walk out of the living room and strut about the house. No one can stop me now. What's he going to do? Lock me up? Been there, done that. There's nothing left he can take from me. I have nothing left to give.

"Where are you going?" he asks.

"Oh, now I can't look around either?" I spit back at him while glancing at him over my shoulder.

He follows me around. "Of course you can. But I wasn't done yet."

"I am," I say, and I go straight for his study. He immediately catches up and blocks my path. "I'd like to explore this room now. Are you going to stop me from doing that too?" A smirk spreads on my face. "Something you'd like to keep hidden?"

He smiles back and then unlocks the door himself. "No ... not at all."

And as the door opens, I step back straight into his office. I only saw a few glimpses of the books in there before. I'm curious to know what kind of things he does here. If this is where he makes all his dirty plans.

"So ... where's that book again?" I murmur, looking around. "The one with all the rules in it. You pass that down from generation to generation, don't you?"

"Where it belongs," he replies, somewhat annoyed, probably because I managed to find all that out from a simple glance last time.

"In the shelves?" I point at the bookcase.

His whole frame tightens. "I don't think that's a good idea."

"Why not?" I ask, raising a defiant brow. "I can't know what it is you do in here?"

His nostrils flare. I know I'm pushing it, but we both know he's going to give me what I want ... because he wants me to be happy. Even if I know I never will be when I'm a prisoner. But he doesn't need to know that.

"I'd rather tell you myself than have you snoop through the pages of that book," he says, folding his arms. "There's some personal information in there."

"Personal like what?"

He sucks in a breath through his nose. "From the other guests."

My eyes widen, and I stop on my way to the bookshelf. "Oh."

I was ready to peek into his business, but I don't want to see into people's private mess. All the people who came here before me must've felt super guilty about their sins. No need for me to add to that.

"So what else is there then?" I ask, letting my hand slide along the laptop. "Is this where you check all the cameras?"

When he nods, my skin begins to prick. I turn and open it up, but the login screen is blocked by a password, of course.

"So I'm guessing this is where you watched me, huh?" I murmur. "While I was naked in my room ... or sliding into the tub ... Did you touch yourself while watching me?"

When I turn on my heels, he's right there, mere inches away from me, a dead-sexy grin on his face. The palms of his hands land on the desk beside me, trapping me between him and the laptop. "I'm sure you'd like to know that ... wouldn't you?"

My whole body begins to bubble with heat, but I ignore it by blowing off some steam and running out from underneath his trap before he does something that will make me want to slap him.

He quickly closes the laptop again while I snatch up the frame on his desk again. "Is this your mother?"

He nods, though the look in his eyes is anything but filled with love.

"What happened to her?" I ask.

He steps toward me again and grabs a strand of my hair, tucking it behind my ear. "If I tell you … will you indulge in my wish as well?"

I gulp. Is knowing this information worth the price? "Depends on what it is."

"Well, you're asking me very personal information about my life …" He cocks his head. "There's a hefty price."

My eyes narrow as I look into his. The look he gives me full of hunger and longing, the type that would make any woman's knees buckle.

He leans into my ear. "But you've already decided that you want to know, haven't you?" he whispers. "You're too curious about my past to say no."

He's right.

I couldn't say no, even if I wanted to.

Because if nothing else is given to me, then I want to know why.

I want to know what makes this man tick.

So I nod. "Fine. Tell me."

A devilish smirk forms on his face, one that only predicts trouble. And he leans in once again only to whisper something that almost makes me drop the frame. "Bend over on the desk."

# SEVENTEEN

## Eli

Her face is priceless. The kind of toxic love I enjoy very much. She hates me for telling her what I want from her, but she hates herself even more for saying yes.

Because she knows as well as I do she's not going to back down from this.

She might have, before she fell into my clutches, but ever since she's been with me she's blossomed into a beautiful, self-indulging flower that knows exactly what she wants and is ready to get it.

She wants to know more about me? Fine, I'll give it to her … exactly the way I want to. And it will cost her her body.

She throws me a dirty look but then turns around, exactly as expected. The grin is almost plastered to my face.

Finally, I have her exactly where I want her, willing and

needy.

Maybe it's dirty for me to trade sex for information, but she knew what she was getting herself into when trying to persuade me. And I'm never opposed to giving her body some much-needed love.

Who knows, maybe she will soften up to me a little and forget all the conundrum about me wanting to make her my wife and make her have my baby.

She positions herself on the side of the desk, her perky ass sticking up beautifully from underneath that bright yellow dress that fits snugly on her body. And I cannot wait to peel it all away until there's nothing left but her naked skin begging for my touch.

I revel at the moment, my cock already hard as fuck just from the view.

I push myself up against her, my bulge nudging against her flesh, making her squeeze her legs together. She holds the desk while her head rolls sideways.

"So what are you planning to do, huh?" she asks.

My hand slides up and down her back until goose bumps appear on her skin.

I know she wants to deny our attraction, but it's no use. I know what she feels for me. I know she wants me just as much as I want her, and no amount of hatred can get in the way of that.

"Whatever I choose ..." I groan with delight at the thought of making her beg for my cock.

But I don't think I can wait that long.

I push up the dress until her bare pussy is exposed, my fingers immediately diving in. She holds her breath, almost as if to hide a moan.

"This pussy misses me, doesn't it?" I muse, toying around with her clit until she's wet and dripping.

"No," she hisses. "And you'd better not try. If you try to shove your cock in, this agreement will end." She looks at me with such furor in her eyes that I'm amazed.

*Fine. If she wants to play it that way …*

I smack her ass, and a squeal leaves her mouth. "Fine. Have it your way."

I open the locked drawer and quickly take out the private collection of toys I keep only to please her. There's a bunch of them, but today I'm only interested in one thing.

The plug.

Her eyes widen at the sight of it. "What are you going to do?"

A dirty smile forms on my lips. "If I can't fuck you in the pussy … then I guess I'm going to have to enjoy your other orifices."

The realization of what's about to happen really settles in with her, but still, she doesn't budge. Even when her body shivers on the table as I plant my hand on her naked back, my hand hovering near her ass.

"Are you going to …"

I grab the lube from the desk and spread it all over the toy. "Yes, I'm going to stuff you with this instead."

But I don't shove the toy into her pussy.

Instead, I slap her ass once and then push the tip against her ass.

She gasps, a loud moan leaving her mouth when I push it inside.

"Don't fight it," I groan, slowly pushing it farther and farther.

"Oh my God, what ... Oh, God," she murmurs, barely able to contain herself. "It's so tight."

When it's in, the sparkling jewel on the backside makes me groan with pleasure. I smack her ass again for good measure, and she bounces along with the rhythm as if she enjoys it.

"Hmm ... You're getting a taste for it, aren't you?" I ask.

"Shut up," she growls, making me laugh. "I'm only doing this so you will give me more information."

"Right." I roll my eyes and take a deep breath.

*Keep telling yourself that, little angel.*

I slap her butt again just to hear that little squeak that sounds like music to my heart. I love it when she's trying to hide her excitement. But when my fingers slide down toward her pussy, it's already dripping.

"Of course you are," I add.

Before she can reply, I go to my knees in front of the desk and bury my head between her legs. They tighten at first, locking me in a grip between her knees. But after my tongue begins to twist around her pussy and circle her clit, they relax again.

Even if she thinks she's going to squeeze my head off … she can't actually push herself to do it.

She loves it too much. She loves what I do to her, how I can make her burn with desire, how I can make her say things she thought she'd never say … how I can make her beg.

And when that particular moan leaves her mouth, I know she's about ready to commit.

When she's about to come, I pull away again, leaving her pussy wet and swollen.

"Oh … fuck," she mutters, completely unraveling on that desk.

A rumbling grunt forms in the back of my throat. "You didn't think I'd let you get off that easily, did you?"

Her nose twitches, seething anger in her eyes. "I thought you only had sex with people to make them confess?"

"No … not when it comes to the girl we pick," I reply, my hand landing on her ass again. "And I know exactly what I want."

I zip down my pants and pull out my cock, which is hard as a rock and bouncing up and down at the sight of her wet and half-naked on my desk. I leisurely apply some lube, as I can't wait any longer to ravage her. But if she won't have me in her because she's afraid we'll make babies, I know the perfect solution.

I pull the toy from her ass so fast that it makes a long-drawn-out moan escape her lips. And before she even realizes it, I push the tip inside and slowly ease into her ass.

Her lips form an o-shape as another groan comes out the deeper I go.

Once I'm fully in, another animalistic moan falls off her tongue, and my cock hardens inside her from the sound. I pull out and go back in again, my pace increasing every time as she gets used to the feel of having me inside her.

The longer it goes on, the hornier we both get, until I can no longer stop myself from fucking her like the little sinner she is. Every time I thrust in and out of her, she buckles against the desk. Her shoes drop off the moment I spank her hard. She tiptoes around, trying to find balance while I rail her from behind, but I don't even care. I'm taking what's mine.

I thrust in, and she squeals again. "It feels so full."

"Good. That's what you deserve for trying to spite me," I reply, going deeper and deeper with every stroke.

With my free hand, I slide along her still sensitive pussy, which makes her push up against the desk. Especially when I shove a finger inside. I love to see her squirm for me.

I circle around her clit all while fucking her ass, seeing her unravel more and more until her moans come out in short gasps, her eyes almost rolling into the back of her head.

Right then, I bury myself deep inside.

She comes hard, her pussy dripping with sweet wetness as I play with it while she falls apart. The dirtiness of it pushes me over the edge, and I let myself go inside her. I clutch her ass with both hands as my seed jets into her, filling her to the brim. The groan that follows is nothing short of animalistic.

The sheer force of my orgasm is so tremendous that I want to pounce down on top of her, so I do. My mouth opens up, and I plant sweet, delectable kisses all over her back, the salty taste of sweat mixing with my saliva, making my dick bounce up and down with excitement while it's still inside her.

However, she suddenly pushes herself off the desk and steps aside so hard that I'm forced to pull back my dick and my fingers. Panting, she pats down her dress and glares at me.

"Don't … kiss me," she hisses. "That wasn't a part of the agreement."

I frown, taken aback by her sudden need to hate me again, even though she very much wanted me to fuck her just now. Still, it stings when she says that.

But I swallow down my pride. "Fine. I got a little carried away."

She keeps staring at me, her eyes sometimes wavering a little bit to ignore my nakedness. But I don't mind. She wants to gawk? Have at it. I'm all hers.

She swiftly snatches some tissues out of the box on my desk and cleans herself up, throwing them into the bin like she's saying goodbye to literally everything that even remotely reminds her of me. Like she's trying to make this clinical, but it's not going to work.

"I've held my end of the deal. Now it's your turn," she

says.

I raise a brow. Well, that's one way to get to the point.

Sighing out loud, I tuck in my dick, unable to hide my disappointment. "Fine. You want to know what happened to my *mother*?"

I can't say I enjoy talking about it, but if she really wants to know all there is to know about me, I guess I have no choice. After all, I want her to trust me again.

So I look her dead in the eyes when I say, "My father murdered her."

Shock makes her eyes grow big.

"I'm not done yet," I say, as I throw a look at the woman in the picture on my desk.

The woman who hated me so much that she wished she never had me.

But that woman was the catalyst for what I am today.

Along with Amelia.

\*\*\*

**Ten years ago**

Despite the fact that I know what my father does for a living, I'm still horrified to watch him dig a grave for the man he just killed.

It wasn't intentional. Or at least, that's what he told me.

But the man refused to confess, and the harder my father pushed with punishments, the less the man began to care. And it enraged my father, made him boil over until he could no longer stop himself.

And I watched him do it.

I watched him hit that man with an ax until the blood squirted all over the walls of the basement.

Until his squeals died out, and there was nothing left but the ragged breaths of my father.

I long knew he was capable of violence.

But I never realized just how deep it went.

Just how far he'd go if something didn't go his way.

My father stops digging for a moment, only to give me a stare laced with anger. I swallow as he approaches me and hits me against the back of the head.

"You are just gonna stand there and do nothing all day, huh?" he growls, smacking me again. "You disappointing fuck. Get moving!"

He pushes the shovel into my hand and shoves me forward so hard that I almost fall over right into the grave myself. All he does is laugh. "You're pathetic."

I throw him a look and start digging, even though my conscience is weighing down on me.

Every day, my father steps further and further away from the rules that govern our house. No longer does he wait until someone actually commits a sin, until someone is brought in front of us by their family.

No, he just picks people up from the streets and then makes up some sort of story as to why they deserve it.

After all, everyone is a sinner, deep down. Everyone

deserves to be punished.

Even him.

The longer I dig, the more I'm beginning to realize that he's never paid for his.

For all the hurt he's inflicted on his sinners.

All the pain he's inflicted on me.

All the suffering he made my mother endure.

"Can you even do one thing correctly?" he growls while towering over me from behind.

Even though I'm doing the best that I can, it's still not enough for him. It never will be. This man will never be satisfied. He will never quit.

I pause for a moment while digging, taking a few deep breaths.

"You will never be able to take over if you just give up like that," he says.

"Did it ever occur to you I might not want to?"

I don't know why I say it, but I do. I can't help myself. I've taken so much from him over the years that I don't care anymore.

"Tsk, you're just like your mother. Useless," he says. "But I'll make a man out of you."

His words cut like a knife straight into my heart.

*My mother...*

She may have hated me for existing, but she was still a human being.

And he tormented her so much that she despised being alive to the point of trying to jump.

One month.

That's all she was given after she tried … before he killed her himself with his own bare hands. She was asleep. She couldn't fight him off.

My father's assistant found her cold in the bed, with the markings still clearly visible around her throat.

No one said a word.

Not even me.

How could I when I knew what he was capable of?

When I saw with my own eyes what awaited me if I tried to defy him?

His rage was enough to kill my mother … and even though she hated me, she didn't deserve that fate. She deserved justice.

I thought my father always said that no one is without sin and that sinners deserved to be punished. But did he ever get punished for his crimes?

"She deserved better than you," I say through gritted teeth.

"Who?" he muses.

I'm seething with hatred. "My mother."

He makes a face. "Why do you even care? She hated you."

"Because you made her have me!" I yell, and in that same moment, I spin on my heels and strike him with the shovel.

I didn't mean to hit him so hard.

But his voice and the words he spoke made me want to

strike back at this menace.

It's just like that girl once said at my mother's funeral … Sins never do anyone any good.

When the blade makes contact with his skin, it crushes his skull, and his body flops sideways onto the forest ground. Blood oozes from his nose, mouth, and ears.

Hatred makes people do wretched things.

And it will always breed more hatred in return.

# EIGHTEEN

*Amelia*

**Present**

I'm flabbergasted by his story.

He actually killed his own father for murdering his mother.

And all I can do is stare at him with my mouth wide open.

"I buried him in the same hole on top of the sinner he wanted to bury," he adds.

I swallow. "Is that … out there in the woods in front of the house?"

When he nods, my whole body feels like it's twisted into knots. I can't believe he actually killed people, let alone his father. Well, I knew he said he had killed... but to hear the entire story straight up from his mouth is still hard.

"You must be scared of me now," he says, sighing out loud.

I lower my eyes. "Well ... I did ask for it."

"Right." He folds his arms. "I'm not ashamed of what I did. He deserved it."

I lick my lips. "Because of what he did to your mom?"

"She hated me. But she didn't deserve to die." His nostrils flare as he pauses for a moment. "My father was unfit to rule this House."

"And you are?" I raise a brow.

He steps away from me. "I never claimed I was. But this house has to continue."

"Why?"

"Because there are people out there depending on us," he explains, sucking in a breath. "And I have realized that this place offers a way out for those who have no other choice."

For some reason, that last sentence really ticks me off. "I didn't *have* a choice."

"I know," he says, looking me dead in the eyes.

The conversation grows quiet again.

I don't even know why I wanted to know all this. I guess a part of me is trying to find out the reasons behind all his choices. The reasons for me being here. So I can maybe, maybe understand him a little bit better.

But I realize now that doing so would only mean giving

him more ammo against him. Because understanding a man like him means I have feelings for him, something I cannot allow myself to ever feel, no matter how hard he tries.

So I straighten my shoulders and walk past him. "Thanks for the information."

When I clutch the door handle, he says, "So that's it? You just got what you came for, and now you're leaving?"

"We had a deal. A mutual exchange."

He grabs my arm and forces me to look at him. "Don't tell me it wasn't more than that."

Our eyes connect in a heated battle, one that could strike fear into anyone's heart.

He wants my love, but he knows I will never give it to him. "Sorry, but I'm not going to suddenly change my mind after what you did to me."

His face darkens. "What's it going to take then?"

I jerk my arm loose from his grip. "*Everything.*"

It's the same response he's given me when I asked him what else I needed to do to pay for my sins. But I want him to feel what I felt, to suffer as I did. And I know that's petty … but sometimes being petty is the best way to get a point across.

\*\*\*

**Later that week**

We haven't spoken in days. I don't even know how long I haven't seen him. All I know is that I quite enjoying my free time, lounging about the house. It's a shame I'm not allowed to go outside, though. He's probably scared I'm going to try to run again, even though he has a ton of guards following me around wherever I go.

I rarely have some peace and quiet of my own. But at least it beats having Eli hover around me like he wants to eat me up. It's already tough enough to ignore his stares, let alone when his eyes scream, 'I want to fuck you into oblivion.'

All I know is that he's locked himself inside his study, busy with work or something.

No one will tell me why. When I ask the guards, none reply. I don't dare ask Soren. He scares me a little. And when I asked Tobias when I finally did see him come out of his man-cave, all he did was tell me to ask Eli himself.

But the whole point was to avoid him.

I sigh as I sit down on the staircase and stare up at the ceiling, wondering who made that beautiful painting.

Suddenly, the door to Eli's study opens up. I don't look, but I definitely hear the clicking of shoes on the floor, they're unmistakable his, and they make my heart thump.

He stops near the staircase, and I can feel his eyes practically burning a hole into my skin.

"I know the story I told you was damning, but I wanted

to be truthful with you."

*Because I asked.*

I'm not sure he would've told me if I hadn't made him.

And I don't really think about it a lot.

"Are you going to talk to me?" Eli asks.

I shrug.

There's no point unless I have something to ask, which I don't. He's made his plans very clear. And no story he tells me will change the way I feel about that.

"I know I've been very busy with work these days, but that doesn't mean I don't want to see you."

I don't even respond this time.

After a while, he continues. "Do you hate me so much?"

Again, I don't reply. It should be obvious by now.

He sighs out loud and sits down beside me on the stairs, staring up at the same beautiful painting that's on the ceiling. I almost open my mouth to ask, but then I realize I was ignoring him just to give him a piece of his own medicine.

"I know you're just ignoring me to punish me. And I can tell you that it has worked," he says. "I hate it. I hate not talking to you. I hate not being able to touch you. To kiss you."

The way he says it, with so much emotion that it takes my breath away, hurts my soul.

But I cannot ever let him get close again.

"Amelia ... please," he murmurs. "Tell me why."

"You know why," I rebuke, looking him dead in the eyes.

His nostrils flare. "You want to be salty the rest of your life, fine. But that doesn't mean you should deprive yourself too."

I snort. "I'm not depriving myself of anything. I don't want you."

"Lies," he retorts.

"Lies or not, you still won't get it."

"What do you want from me?" he asks. "I bared my soul to you. I told you all my darkest secrets, and it's still not enough."

"I don't think you have," I reply.

His eyes twitch, narrow, and full-on rage blossoms on his face in the likes I've never seen. He gets up from the stairs, looking down at me. "You want me to be truly honest?"

I gulp at the sight of his powerful frame. With his slick dark brown hair combed back over his head and his navy blue pants along with those brown loafers, he looks like he came walking straight out of a James Bond movie.

But no amount of sexiness can ever fix the corruption hidden underneath, and I must always remember that, even if my body screams to forgive him.

"You want me to show you all my cards?" he asks.

I don't know if it's a rhetorical question or if we're finally getting to the part where he goes on his knees for me. Either way, I tell myself I don't care, so I look away.

"Fine," he adds, his nostrils flaring again from my defiance. "You want to know the full truth? I'll show it to you."

He grabs my arm and pulls me up.

"Hey!" I exclaim. "What is your problem?" I ask as he drags me along. "Where are we going?"

"Somewhere I should've taken you right from the start," he growls.

And he drags me straight toward the stairs that go down to the cellar, the forbidden area, the place I've never seen before. He takes me downstairs, muttering, "Careful with your steps." As if now is the time to be chivalrous. I swallow hard as the lights flicker around me.

The distraction makes me slip on one of the steps, and I shriek. Within seconds, his arms are around my body, clutching me tight to his.

"I said be careful," he growls, though this time a little less enraged.

I blush and push him off me. "Uh, thanks." But even as he turns around again, I can't shake the feeling of his warm embrace. I'm thinking of things I shouldn't be thinking of anymore.

*Stop it, Amelia. You made a promise to yourself, and you're going to stick with it.*

We go down farther and farther until we get to the bottom, where Eli flicks a switch and some not so bright lights turn on, guiding our way through a narrow hallway filled with ancient-looking doors.

"What is this place?" I mutter, looking around. My fingers skim past the stones that line the wall, all of them feeling like they haven't been cleaned in years. This place looks old ... and hellish. Just like he said.

"This was built a long time ago. It's older than the house," he answers as we walk toward a particular door in the back.

"Older than this house?" I frown. I didn't think that was possible, but apparently, it is. "How long has this place existed?"

"A very, very long time," he responds.

I gulp. And all this time, it's remained intact, hiding the things they do from the rest of the world.

"Our ancestors kept the sinners behind these doors," Eli says, and he glances at me over his shoulder with a devilish smirk on his face. "What can I say? They weren't as fond of giving sinners the luxuries they are given today."

I throw him a dirty look, and he smirks and looks away again, which makes me want to jump on his back and strangle him. Trying to make me feel humble about my perceived privileges compared to those kept here is ridiculous.

But then I hear a scream.

I pause and gasp in shock as I glare behind me, wondering where it came from. "What was that?"

Eli waits too and points at one of the doors.

My eyes widen as the realization hits me. "You still keep people here?"

He says nothing. The only thing that moves is his eyebrow, just a twitch, but it's enough.

I move to the door where the sound emanated from and press my ear to the door. Another yowl follows, and I lean back again, sweat dripping down my forehead. I glance at Eli, who is still gazing at me with full intent as though this is what he wanted me to know.

"Go on. Look."

# NINETEEN

*Amelia*

I shiver in place, contemplating whether to take a peek. But my curiosity is too strong for me to ignore, and I peer through the tiny window. A man is strapped upside down to a cross. His genitals are connected to an electrical device that continues to shock him every other minute. He squeals in pain when the trigger goes off again, all automatic.

The man's eyes suddenly land on me, the sheer pain in them catching my breath … because I've seen those eyes before.

He's that man … the one who followed me from Joe's club all the way back to my apartment.

No.

It can't be, can it?

I step away and avert my eyes as I realize what this all means.

"You recognize that man, don't you?" Eli asks.

I can only nod, but the rest of my body feels frozen.

"Hard to witness?"

"Why would anyone do this?" I mutter.

He steps closer while I back away against the wall. "To punish him for his sins ... And I think you know what those are."

*Trying to take me to my own apartment.*

*I told Eli not to kill him, so he brought him here.*

"You didn't think I'd let that fucker get away with what he tried to do to you, did you?" he says through gritted teeth.

"Death would have been an easier way out for him," I murmur.

"Exactly, and he deserves no less than this," Eli responds.

I'm overcome with guilt, shame, and so much more. I wouldn't wish this on anyone—this pain and suffering—yet I can't bring myself to pity the man in front of me. Because to feel sorry for him would mean forgiving him for what he did. And I can't ever let myself forget what he tried.

Just like I couldn't forgive myself for what Chris did to me ... and for what I did to him.

"It's a continuous cycle of guilt," I whisper, tears welling up in my eyes.

He nods slowly, and it feels as though the world is

unraveling before me. "Now you understand."

"Who decides what punishment is given?" I ask in a moment of clarity.

His face darkens and his voice remains emotionless. "I do."

I swallow again. "I thought you kept all of us in those rooms upstairs."

"The ones who deserve nothing get nothing," he responds.

"How do you decide what punishment to give them then?" I ask.

A filthy smirk forms on his lips. "It depends on the person and their sin. Some require solitude or torture … others require sex."

I gulp, thinking about all the ways he made me come, all the ways he got me on my knees, just so I could remember. Seeing that knife resting in the chair that day I finally realized what I'd done; it was all a part of his plan.

I gaze into his eyes, trying to discover what he's thinking, but all I see is my own reflection staring right back at me. I could look away, but I can't.

"Hurts to see, doesn't it?" he asks, placing a hand on the wall right beside me, trapping me inside. "To watch them suffer."

"I don't understand …" *My own emotions* is what I wish to say, but I don't dare to say it out loud for fear of what it means … What it makes me.

"Can you imagine what I've been going through doing

what I do …" He entwines his fingers through my hair, toying with a strand as he inches closer. "To you."

"This is not the same thing," I retort, determined not to succumb to his overbearing presence even though I want nothing more than for him to take me back into the safety of my comfortable little room … where he can fuck me until the sun comes up and goes down again.

But that's exactly why he's doing this. So I'll yield and promise never to escape again. So I'll let him have me and love me. Because this is the alternative.

Because knowing the truth hurts.

But I won't falter.

"Tell me more," I say through gritted teeth.

"What's there to tell?" he muses. "We hurt people for a living. You already knew that."

"Who else was in here?"

He swallows, his tongue briefly dipping out to slide along the edge of his lips, and I can't help but focus on it. "C'mon."

Suddenly, he leans away again, and I'm left panting and with buckling knees. Slapping some sense into myself, I force myself to keep up and follow suit.

He points at another door. "Have a look."

When I do, I see the other man who harassed me at Joe's. The one Eli put a gun to his head. His hands and feet are covered in blood. "Oh my …God."

"God isn't present in these chambers," Eli says.

"No … no wonder why you said this was hell."

It wasn't merely a figure of speech.

"This guy has been here the longest," he says.

"Number seven," I mutter.

"Hmm?"

I quickly look away. "Nothing."

With his brows furrowed, he stares at me for a few seconds. "We only managed to bring the other two in after your escape."

My stomach feels heavy like it's about to turn inside out.

"And now you know what we do," he says.

I turn to face him. "This is what you wanted to show me? What you wanted me to know?" The sting is too much to ignore. "What was your plan? To show me so I'd cower and do what you want? To remind me I could end up here too?"

His pupils dilate, and his body tenses. "No. I would never, *ever*."

"Really?" I put my hands against my side. "Because it sure seemed like that's what you were warning me about."

He cocks his head, rage exploding like a volcano in his eyes. "I did *everything* to keep you away from here. This is Soren's domain. And I do not ever want you in his clutches."

"Soren's domain?" I pause, my lips still parted, but then it hits me. "When Tobias said he wanted me to be punished, this is what he meant, wasn't it?"

When Eli nods, the adrenaline spikes like a drug, making me hyper aware of my environment, and I feel the sudden need to turn around and run.

But Eli's hand suddenly grips my arm tight, digging his fingers into my skin. "I would *never* allow them to lay a finger on you."

Oh. He's saved me now? That's it? That's what this is about?

"And that's supposed to make me feel *safe*?" I scoff, frowning at him. "You still used me like a fuck doll. Like I was nothing more than the sum of my sins. That hurt too."

He sucks on his lip, looking even more riled up than before. "You think I did all those things because I like it? Because I love to see you in pain?" When I spin on my heels, he whips me back around to look at him. His face is full of anguish, and something about it hits me like a brick. "Look at me. Just look. Please."

He's never begged me like that before, and it undoes me, dissolving whatever determination I had.

"I hurt them because I must punish them for their sins …" His hand rises to meet my face, waiting, waiting for me to pull away. When I don't, he softly caresses my cheek. "But anyone who hurt you, especially."

My face softens when he lowers his hand. "You did this for me?"

He gives me a firm nod even though his jaw is clenched tightly and his hand is palmed into a fist.

"You captured and tortured those men—"

"*Because* they hurt you," he says, his words cutting as harshly as his voice. "And I did the same thing to you." His nostrils flare as he sucks in a loud breath. "I hated every single second of it. I hate, *hate* hurting you. But I needed you to see what you had done," he says, his voice aching as much as my heart. "I needed you to see the pain in your own heart. I did it so you could remember and get past it. So you could heal."

He clutches his chest like he's trying to grip his heart while towering over me. "It wounds me. Physically. Emotionally. But it's a toll I accept."

"Why? Why don't you stop all of it?" I ask, feeling out of breath just looking at him.

He's never been this open with me, and the sheer power he exudes is all-consuming.

He lowers his eyes away from mine. "I can't."

The rush of adrenaline feels trapped under a layer of disappointment. "*Why*? Why not?" I grab his hands and clutch them tight, his eyes rising to meet mine in a moment of reinvigoration.

"Because this is what I was born to do," he says.

I never thought I would see it firsthand, but I have never seen this much misery in a living man. And worse is the amount of worry it gives my already aching heart.

"And there is something else I need you to see."

\*\*\*

# ELI

My hand tears away from hers.

For the first time since I laid eyes on her, it's like she's the one chasing me instead of the other way around.

All of our back and forth bickering, the push and pull of our hearts, my devotion to her ... it's all come down to this single moment. The one thing I've kept hidden from her all this time.

It's going to destroy her.

And me along with it.

But I must.

I have no choice.

No more options left to make her see the real me.

Nothing left to give except this ... the full and honest truth.

And I already know exactly how it's going to end.

I hold my breath as I walk toward the door all the way in the back.

A loud squeal coming from the other end of the door makes Amelia stop following me. Her pupils dilate. Finally, she realizes the truth. That wasn't a sound any man could make.

It was a woman's voice.

She rushes past me right as I open the door, only to stop in the midst of her tracks the second she spots who's strapped to that bed with nothing but her own mind to keep her company.

The girl who fucked Chris.

Amelia's lips part, her breath faltering. "This … this is …"

"The woman who Chris betrayed you for. The woman who snaked her way into your bed."

Tears well up in her eyes as she stands frozen to the ground, staring at the woman in front of her, who squeals some more when she sees Amelia. Her mouth has been covered by a thick piece of duct tape, which she would never be able to get off on her own because of her bound wrists and ankles.

"What did you do to her?" Amelia asks.

I frown. "Is that really what you want to ask?"

She makes an uncomfortable face and approaches the woman gently. "I can't …"

"Yes, you can. Go on. Talk to her."

She turns white as a ghost. "But she's—"

I march past Amelia and rip the tape off the woman's lips. The woman shrieks. "There."

"You asshole!" She tries to punch and kick me, but it's futile. The straps are way too tightly wrapped around her skin. "Let me go!"

Amelia looks at the woman from a safe distance, her whole body shaking.

"What do you want from me?" the woman asks. "Tell me!"

I clutch her chin and force her to look at me. "I don't

want anything from you." I push her head so she looks at Amelia. "But *she* does."

Amelia gasps, her pupils dilating. "I ... I ..."

"Who are *you*?" the woman barks.

"My name's ... Amelia," she mutters, completely shaken.

I block Amelia's view and lift her chin so her gaze meets mine. "Now is your chance to ask whatever is on your mind. No questions are off-limits."

"Why? Why did you do this?" she murmurs.

The question catches me off guard. Not because I didn't expect her to ask it. I did. But because I thought the first thing on her mind would be to find out why the woman would have sex with a married man.

"I did this for you," I answer, lowering my head. "Because she *hurt* you. And she deserves this."

"Did you do the same thing to her as you did to me?" she asks, swallowing as though the question itself pains her.

My eyes narrow. "You mean ... sex?" I shake my head. "I don't want any other woman, Amelia. Only you."

"What the hell are you two going on about?" the woman asks. "Let me go!"

Amelia looks at her over my shoulder before returning her attention to me. "So what then ... torture?"

I raise my brows. "No. She's an escort. A woman like her requires ... a particular kind of punishment." I sigh. "Sex only works on those who are deprived."

Amelia's cheeks flush. Even though I was not talking

about her, I guess in a sense I was.

"She was not deprived of that. Nor would pain work on a woman like her who is so eager to please," I say. "She requires solitude. Complete and utter silence can break even the most spirited souls."

"So you kept her here tied up all by herself for how long?" she asks. I close my eyes for a second, at which point Amelia already fills it in for me. "Long enough to go insane."

I won't deny it. "It's what she deserves."

"No one does," she hisses back.

"The woman fucked your lover," I retort, pointing at the woman bound to the bed. "Look at her. Ask her if she cares."

Amelia's eyes are seething, and she looks fuming, but at the same time, there is also something else looming in the background. Defeat.

Her shoulders rise and fall, and she passes me by, holding up the back of her hand instead of shoving me aside to signify that she's done talking with me. And I watch her as she approaches the woman, whose eyes are red and filled with madness.

"Do you remember me?" Amelia asks.

"No, I don't know who—"

"I was the girl who looked down at you through the window. The one who saw you kiss Chris. Do you remember him?"

Her brows furrow, but then her eyes widen, and shock

riddles her face. "You—"

"You made my man cheat on me," Amelia says, tears staining her eyes. "And I ... I ..."

The woman suddenly says, "Look, I didn't know he was married."

"Married?" Amelia murmurs. "No, we weren't ... but you didn't ..."

"No! I didn't know!" she exclaims. "When we hooked up, he said he was single. Besides, this is my job. This is what I do."

"I didn't think he'd ever go look for a hooker," Amelia says, looking down at her feet. "That I was worth so little to him."

"He never even mentioned your name," the woman says.

"What's yours?" Amelia suddenly asks.

"Tiffany," she replies.

Amelia snorts, shaking her head. I don't know if she's laughing or crying ... or both.

"Why?" Tiffany asks.

The look on Amelia's face twists into something I've never seen before. "So I can remember the face and the name of the woman who destroyed my world."

"What?" Tiffany mutters as Amelia gets up, decidedly not about to free her. "No, wait. Don't go. Please. Don't leave me. I've been alone for so long. You don't understand. Please!" She keeps begging, but Amelia keeps walking with her hands clenched into firm fists.

"Please! I beg you. I'm sorry. Please, I'm so sorry," the woman cries out. "It wasn't my choice. *He* made me."

My heart drops ten feet below the ground.

Amelia's ears perk up.

Her head tilts back to Tiffany while I clench my fists.

This is it.

This is the moment when everything comes crashing down on me.

When my world comes to an end.

"*HE* told me to do it." Amelia looks at Tiffany … whose finger is pointed right at me. "He did this to me."

"What?" Amelia murmurs to her.

"That devil over there paid me to do it. He paid me to seduce and fuck Chris."

There it is.

The one and only single truth … and my downfall all wrapped into one sinful sentence.

# TWENTY

## ELI

**The night of the murder**

After I saw those bruises on Amelia's skin, I knew exactly what kind of fucker her boyfriend really was. I thought about going up to his apartment to shoot him in the face multiple times, but only my greed stopped me from doing just that. Because if I shot her boyfriend, she would hate me forever, no matter the reason.

Instead, I've been waiting out here near her apartment, waiting until he would hurt her again so I could step in.

I stare up at the apartment window, through which I can see the pig watching football on his TV while his girlfriend is off partying at some club, trying to drown in her sorrow. What a fucking waste of space.

I will wait until the end of time if I have to, but I will

catch this fucker in his sin, and I will make him pay for his crimes.

Twenty minutes later, he suddenly walks to his door. I don't see him, but I know it went off. Within minutes, he's right back at the couch ... kissing the same woman who Amelia saw him with. Tiffany.

My fingers dig into the leather seat below me.

It takes every ounce of my self-control not to intervene.

He doesn't deserve to fuck anyone, let alone Amelia.

Yet for some reason, she still fell for this disgusting pig.

He's fucking around with Tiffany in the bedroom. I can tell from where the lights switched on and off. I can briefly make out two figures through the blinds before everything goes dark.

I wait in my car, watching the apartment closely for any sign of movement. In the middle of the night, Amelia suddenly comes home. She's wobbling on her feet, clearly intoxicated as hell.

I frown, watching her as she stumbles into the building, wondering if I should follow her. But something tells me that she needs to see this for herself. She needs to know what kind of man her boyfriend really is.

After a while, the lights go on again.

I peer up through the night sky.

Chris comes out of the bedroom, but then he moves into a spot I can't see from where I'm at. The sheer pressure of the moment is making me bite my nails.

A panicked squeal follows mere minutes later.

Adrenaline switches on, and I instantly open the car door and rush out, speeding across the road to get to the other side. I swiftly make it into the building and run up the stairs, not giving a shit about the slow elevator. I go up to the apartment and run toward the door, which appears unlocked ... only to come to a complete, almost-screeching halt.

Right in front of a dead body.

My eyes widen.

Blood pools everywhere.

But it isn't Amelia lying there.

It's Chris.

And Amelia is nowhere to be seen.

A woman wearing only an oversized shirt suddenly stumbles out of the bedroom.

*Tiffany.*

I immediately march toward her. Right as she opens her mouth to squeal, I cover it with my hand.

"Shh ..."

Her eyes grow big. "It's you."

"Yes, it's me," I reply. I guess she didn't expect to see me here. "But I didn't expect to see you here. Did you really have to go that far?"

Her panicked eyes flick back and forth between me and the body.

"Chris," she murmurs. "I didn't do this."

"I know. He's gone. Now keep quiet. I don't want to alert the neighbors or her landlord," I say. "So when I remove my hand, you're going to sit on that couch and wait. Is that understood?"

Only after she nods do I release her from my grasp.

"Oh my God, oh my God," she mutters, tiptoeing around like she's afraid she's going to mess up a crime scene.

But I won't ever let this become one.

Because doing so would mean letting Amelia fall into the hands of the cops, and that's the last thing I want.

There is only one thing that can fix this. Only one thing I can do to make this go away.

With a sigh, I grab my phone from my pocket and dial the number I only call in the biggest of emergencies. "Hey. I need a cleanup crew now. I'll text the address." I quickly end the call and send a text as I promised, making sure to note how much time they're going to get.

It's not much, but it'll have to do. I don't know where she went or when she'll be back, but this place needs to be spotless when she arrives.

Wherever she is right now, she can't be far. She'll eventually come back to see what happened.

Oh, Amelia. If I had known you would go this far to protect yourself, I would've intervened much sooner. If only I knew just what kind of monster you kept hidden inside that precious angel heart of yours.

Maybe I could've stopped you from becoming a sinner.

***

# Amelia

**Present**

*Hate.*

It's such a simple word, but it really isn't enough to describe the mountain of emotions flooding my veins.

I thought I knew what it meant.

That I felt it deep in my bones for this woman who so happily kissed and fucked my boyfriend in my own house.

But to hear her say those words, those awful, mind-numbing words, unravel me.

Something inside me clicks into place. Something I've been feeling for so long but couldn't quite put into words.

And the fear rippling over my back turns to shock while my whole body is beginning to shake irrationally.

I *knew*. Even before she said it, I knew somewhere deep down that this was the all-encompassing truth. The truth Eli tried so hard to keep hidden from me. The truth that would lay bare his gravest sin.

He was the catalyst. The reason for Chris to cheat … and why I lost myself and killed him.

My lip quivers as I turn slowly, shuddering at the mere thought of having to look him in the eye and ask him if it's true. But when our eyes connect, the pure misery deep within his stops me from having to ask anymore.

"It's true," I murmur, tears welling up in my eyes.

Eli's hands tighten into fists as his hooded eyes darken and almost seem to disappear behind a swathe of hair falling down. I thought I had felt the worst emotion there was. That I hated him more than anything, and that was it. But this? The fact that he can't even look at me? That's even worse.

"*This* is what you were trying to hide from me," I say through gritted teeth, pointing at Tiffany, who is still lying there tied to the bed like it's the most normal thing in the world.

"I wasn't trying to hide it," he says, his fists still clenched. He gazes up at me for a brief second. "It's why I brought you here."

"Oh, so *she* could tell me what you did instead of it coming from your own mouth?" I bark.

"You wanted the truth," he says with pain in his eyes. "Now you know."

I shake my head, desperate to keep the tears at bay. "I can't believe this."

I march off, past him, and up the stairs. I don't want to stay for another second.

However, Eli comes rushing after me.

"Amelia, wait!" he says.

"No!" I yell back, running up the stairs to the comfort of the light coming from the ceiling. I know I'm still locked in here, but anything is better than that dark, damp hell down there.

"I know I did something unforgivable," Eli says.

"You know what I did!" I scream, unable to keep myself from spinning on my heels to throw him a deadly glare. "I *killed* him."

My words echo through these halls, but I'm no longer ashamed of them. I know what I've done. I've come to terms with that fact, and I've atoned for my sins.

But *he* hasn't.

I can't help but march straight to him and shove my fingers into his chest. "Because of what *you* did."

He grabs my finger but keeps it there, pointed at his chest. "I did not *make* you kill him. But I am a monster. I know that."

Rage becomes me as my teeth clench together, and the world turns red in front of my eyes.

And I slap him. Hard.

It doesn't register until the sting of my hands shows on his skin.

I stare for a moment as he brings his free hand to his cheek and touches the spot. My finger inches back from his chest as my whole body drifts away.

"I ..." I mutter, unable to put into words what I feel.

I'm sorry, but I'm not sorry, and for that, I'm not sorry either. It's too confusing, too fucked up.

"I deserved that," he says, as though he wants to make it easy on me.

I feel like a snake right now, wishing I could bite him and fill him with the poison he made me endure. "Yes, you did. You don't even deny doing what she said."

"There's no point," he replies.

"So it's the truth," I say. It's not a question, again. "You hired her to fuck Chris."

He clutches the stair railing, squeezing the wood so tight I swear it's going to crack. "Yes."

It hurts so much. It hurts beyond imagination. So much that I didn't see the pain coming until it was too late.

"How could you?" I whisper, saying words I wished I never had to say out loud. "Why?"

His face contorts, his jaw clenching almost as hard as his fists around the wood, the look in his eyes almost too painful to bear. Like he's torn in two. "Out of greed. Because I was selfish. Because I wanted you … all to myself."

My heart aches so badly right now. Why? I don't understand.

"I saw how he treated you," he says, the words coming out with such disgust like he wants to vomit. "How he made you feel. How he *hurt* you. And I couldn't stand it."

My brows furrow. "So you gave him a whore?" I scoff.

He takes a few steps toward me, and I back away. "I gave him a piece of his own medicine … the pain he inflicted on you right back at him."

"But he never knew I saw him!" I yell back.

Eli stops in his tracks right in front of me. "No."

"But that wasn't the point," I mutter. "You ... you wanted me to *kill* him?"

He suddenly looks directly into my eyes. "*No.*"

"Tell me that wasn't the plan," I hiss.

"It wasn't. It was supposed to make you see him for the disgusting piece of shit he really was. So that you'd ... hurt him. But I didn't think you'd go that far."

My nostrils flare. "But it *was* a trap."

His hands turn to fists again. "I couldn't ... have you."

Something twists at my insides. "You asshole!" I yell, slamming both my hands into his chest. "You *made* me sin just so you could bring me here!"

I punch and punch, all while screaming my lungs out like a madwoman, but nothing seems to faze him. He just stands there, head between his shoulders, like a lost dog with his tail between his legs. All because I caught him in the biggest lie.

"Why won't you fight back?" I growl as the tears begin to roll down my face.

"Because this is my punishment," he says.

I pause, midway into swinging on him again, and it feels as though my lungs suddenly can't inhale oxygen anymore.

"For hurting you."

Tears stream down my face. Out of all the vile emotions I expected to feel right now, regret was not one of them. I didn't think I could feel anything for him ... but dammit, I was wrong. And now the regret for ever letting myself fall for a man like this is finally setting in.

"Do what you want to do with me," he says, holding out his hands like he's inviting me in. "Hurt me. Choke me. Kill me."

I step back, unraveling from his touch. "No." I shake my head even when he approaches. "No, I will not play along with your game."

"But this is what I deserve," he says. "After everything I did, don't you want me to pay?"

I nod slowly even though it feels wrong. "I do, but not like this."

"Then how?" he asks, his voice cracking as much as my resolve did when I let him fuck me. "I am yours."

No. He's not mine. He never was.

He only belonged to this house. His own sins.

They'll be his undoing.

"I lov—"

I raise a finger. "Don't. Don't say that word. It isn't true."

"It is. All I did was for you. To save you from him and from yourself," he says. "I did it because I wanted you to be whole again. I wanted you to stand for yourself. And look at you." The smile on his face is like a smack in the face. "You've become so strong."

"Stop," I hiss. "I don't want to hear it."

He swallows. "Amelia …"

"No." I walk toward the stairs, but he grabs my arm.

"Please …"

It's the second time he's said that word, and it still hits

me in the gut and forces me to look at him. But that pain in his eyes is too much to bear. I don't want it to wound my already broken heart even further.

"I need you," he says.

"Should've thought of that before and told me the truth right from the very start ..." I growl, and I tear my arm out of his grip and march upstairs to my bedroom.

Even though it's still in this wretched house, at least that one room is my sanctuary, my temporary haven away from the crazy. Away from him.

And if escaping this monster of a lie means locking myself in my room forever, then I'll do just that.

But halfway across the stairs, my head suddenly begins to spin, and my whole body feels heavier than the wood beneath my feet. My sight as well as my muscles falter, causing me to collapse.

Right into Eli's arms.

After which, everything fades into black.

# TWENTY-ONE

## ELI

I only just managed to catch her in time before she fell. I didn't want her to land head-first against the stairs and get hurt. I know my actions have hurt her all the same, but I could never live with myself if she was hurt beyond repair.

Despite everything I did to her, I care about her. I always did, even when I told myself I didn't. Even when I twisted the truth to make it seem more palatable. I didn't just deceive her, but I deceived myself for a long time.

When I first found her, I wanted her to hurt the same way I was as that boy who lost the mother who never cared about him. That same boy who then murdered his own father just to prove how much he wanted to be loved, how much he cared about his mother, even when she did not.

That same boy always remembered the words that little girl said.

*Hate is a sin.*
*Everyone is here to do good.*
*I just had to believe in myself.*
So I did.

I believed in myself to make the wrong things in this world right again.

I took her words to heart and wielded them as a weapon of justice.

But it cost me the only thing I cared so much about.

Her love.

I sit by my bed in which Amelia lies, still resting like Sleeping Beauty. But my kisses wouldn't wake her up because they'd poison her already weakened soul.

I did this.

I made her endure pain beyond imagination.

I did it because when I first found her after all those years, I blamed her. I blamed her for loving her parents, for putting ideas into my head. And I wanted her to be perfect. This image of her inside my head was that of a perfect human being, spotless, clean, sinless in every way.

And it felt so damn wrong … that I had to crush that image by making her sins a reality.

By forcing her to commit a crime.

But I never realized Chris had already pushed her so far.

That he would make her do something even she had not anticipated. Something so bad she forced herself to forget just so she could cope.

And I couldn't let her go to jail for it.

Instead, I did what I had always done with any sinner.

I brought her here, into my lair, just to punish her for her sins.

Just so I could tell myself she deserved it.

Just so I could make her whole ...

So I could make her mine.

And by doing so, I lost the most valuable thing she ever gave me: Her trust.

I clench my fists and lower my head between my shoulders, muttering some words no one should hear. Right then, a groan emanates from her body, and I look up. Her eyes flutter, and I reach for her hand.

"Amelia. I'm here," I whisper.

Her cold hand instantly retracts. She chooses her cold hands over the warmth I could give her, and it stings. "What happened?"

"You fainted," I say. "I'll get a doctor."

"No," she says, and she quickly crawls against the headboard.

I reach for her again, but she retracts her hand. "Please, let me help you."

"I don't trust you," she says, the words as frigid as ice injected straight into the veins.

"I know you don't ..." I swallow. "But I am still asking you to please let me help you. I am begging you."

"Why should I?" she hisses, and she looks away. "I only fainted."

"It could be something bad," I say.

She folds her arms. "So? Don't pretend you care."

"I do," I say.

"If you did, you wouldn't have wanted to make me sin," she retorts.

The pain in my heart only grows and grows. "That's true. I did do that to you. I won't lie about it. It's why I brought you down into that old dungeon so you could hear it from Tiffany's mouth instead," I say, licking my lips.

"Why would you?"

"Because you asked for the truth, and I wanted to give it to you. I owed you that much," I say. "And I am embarrassed and ashamed, and I know none of it is right. And I have no justification. I was selfish and greedy." I grab her arm. "I was wrong. And I apologize."

Her face contorts as she mulls over my words. "Why are you telling me this? What do you want from me? You think I can forgive you just like that?"

"No, I—"

"I murdered someone, Eli," she says through gritted teeth. "And yes, I know that was my own choice, that I made that decision, somehow. But you made him cheat on me just so I would see what a dickhead he was."

I lower my head and let the hair drape over my eyes again as I don't want her to see the agony poisoning me from the inside out. "I know. I did all that. I wanted you to sin so I could bring you in."

"So you could break me," she says.

I look up into her eyes. "So I could make you mine."

"That's not what you told me when you first brought me here," she hisses.

I suck in a breath. "Because I was lying to myself. Because I blamed you for the fact that I murdered my own father for what he had done to both my mother and me."

She stares at me in shock. "So you ... wanted me to feel the same thing?"

I slowly nod. "I was blinded by hatred, and it was wrong."

None of it was right, and I know that now. I only pretended it was so I could feel good about what I was doing. So I could ignore the feelings I had for her growing underneath the surface of my monstrous skin. That same skin that bears the scars of all these sins I committed just to punish others for theirs.

I am no better than any of them.

"I'm sorry ..." I say. "And I don't expect you to forgive me."

"Good, because I won't," she claps back, and she turns her head away from me, sealing the deal.

I look away too as tears well up in my eyes. The very thing I wished to avoid still happened.

She hates me.

She hates me as much as my mother hated my father.

Her lips part. "What are you going to do with Tiffany?"

"Tiffany?" I'm surprised she'd ask about her. "I wanted to punish her for her sin."

"You already have." Her words are as stark as her face.

"Just like the other women."

I frown, confused as to why she would care so much, especially about the woman who hurt her so badly. "Don't you want to see her punished? You hate the woman."

Her face contorts. "I hate her with all my guts. But there's been enough pain already. Let her go."

I swallow. "I—"

"I don't want to hear any more excuses," she interjects. "Let. Everyone. Go."

I'm amazed. She's asked it so many times before, and I continued to say no, yet she never stops. But more importantly, she doesn't want anyone else to get hurt. Not even the woman who deserves it the most.

I sigh out loud and tap my foot as I stare at the wall. Maybe there is a way for me to make amends. A way to fix everything I've broken. A way to ... make her somewhat happy again.

It will cost me everything.

For a long time, I wasn't willing to pay the price.

I am now.

There is nothing left for me to gain.

Not when Amelia hates me so much she can't stomach the sight of me.

"I know you can't do it. So consider us over," she says. "I don't want anything to do with you anymore."

Her words cut me more than any knife ever could.

I know I've lost her love.

I knew it since the moment I took her down to the

basement.

But she needed to know the whole truth and the extent of my lies ...

I just pray she will find it in her heart to forgive me one day.

I close my eyes for a second and take a deep breath. There are only two other things that must be done. "I won't ask you to do it for me, but please do it for you. Please, let my doctor check you out and make sure you're okay."

She only sighs loudly. "Fine."

Her answer is crude, but it tempers the storm razing my heart momentarily.

I nod and get up from the seat. "I ... I'll go get her."

I walk toward the door, pausing with my hand resting on the handle. "I still want to say this to you. I will never, ever take back this truth: I care deeply about you. From the moment we first met, I knew that we would meet again. You were too special. Too perfect. And when I finally found you ..." I grunt, clenching my fist at the thought of all the things I wish to say. "Every single second of the day I spend thinking about you and all the beautiful faces you make, about all the pain you've been through that made you as resilient as you are now, and about how much of a good woman you really are. And that I do not deserve you. No matter how much I degraded you, no matter how much I tried to climb up that ladder of justice, I could never get even an inch closer to the saint that you are."

She stares up at me, her eyes big, confusion settling in.

"And the longer I spend staring at you, the more I realize how grave the error of my ways. Because I see the pain I inflicted in you now. I am the devil who clipped the angel's wings."

***

## Amelia

Even as he's long disappeared through the door, I can't help but stare at it, wondering when he'd come back or if he'd come back at all. But more importantly, because I wanted him to stay. I wanted him to tell me all the things he had never said to me before, about the beauty underneath all this pain I've suffered, about the ways that I remind him of all the good in the world. I wanted him to fight. I wanted him to beg.

I wanted him to feel just an inkling of everything I have since the moment he took me. Since the moment I began to fall.

When he said he clipped the angel's wings, it undid something inside me, unfurling some of the coils that had twisted around my heart even after all these horrendous things he's done.

A part of me wanted to forgive.

Even if I know damn well he doesn't deserve it.

And I know I would never say the words out loud.

Deep down, I still wanted to be given the opportunity. Because he gave it to me too.

I sigh to myself as I look away and groan to myself when I smell the scents coming off this bed. *His* bed, which still smells just as intoxicating as he did. I slap my hands in front of my face so I don't have to look at or smell any of it anymore. Everything around me reminds me of him.

I hate this. I hate how much I hate him. Because I didn't *want* to hate him, but he made me anyway. But what I hate most of all is how he made me feel so many things ... He made me feel wanted. He made me feel like I was needed. Like I meant something to him.

And that destroys me.

Fifteen minutes later, someone knocks on the door, and I'm pulled from my thoughts. A woman sticks her head inside. "Hi there, you're Amelia, right?"

I nod. "Who ... who are you?"

"Audrey. I'm Eli's doctor," she says as she gets inside, clutching a small bag.

"Oh." I didn't expect Eli, out of all the people, to have a female doctor. Then again, I know the women here would probably need one often. Maybe that's why.

"You probably expected a man, right?" she muses as she grabs a chair.

"Sorry." My face turns red.

She laughs. "No worries. Happens all the time. I

consider it a compliment."

"I'm amazed Eli would hire a woman," I say. "You know what he does, right?"

She nods as she puts the chair down beside the bed. "I know he makes people confess their sins if that's what you mean."

"And you're okay with it?" I ask as she grabs my arm.

"Yes." She puts a band around it to measure my blood pressure. "And I know the people he does it to deserve it."

I make a face. "So you think *I* deserve to be here?"

"I don't know what you did," she says as she listens to my heart. "But I know that his heart is in the right place."

A tsk escapes my mouth. "Eli? He has no heart. Never did."

"If that was true, then why would he help all these people atone?" she murmurs as she checks my pulse.

"For the money," I quip.

She raises a brow. "Did he get paid for you?"

I swallow. Hard. Apparently, she knows more than she lets on.

She is right, though. He didn't get a dime, not from me or from anyone in my life. Maybe he did it because he wanted me. After all, he was selfish and needed me to be his.

And I don't know why but my entire body erupts into goose bumps when that thought passes through my mind.

"Anyway … your lungs sound good, but your blood pressure is a bit low. You should take it slow in the coming days. See if you perk up a bit."

"So … nothing's wrong?" I mutter as she puts her stuff back into her little bag.

"Not that I can see," she says, shrugging. "But take it easy because it could be an infection, that sort of thing. Hopefully, it will clear up in a few days."

"Oh, right," I mutter as she gets up and marches back to the door. "So that's it?"

"That's it." She smiles. "But if you need me, have Eli call me, and I'll be right up. I live on this island too, so it's easy to get here."

Aha. Interesting. So I guess she works only for him then. No wonder his work sounded so easy to her. She's used to it. Maybe she's worked with him for years.

"Just get some sleep and rest up, okay?" she says as she opens the door. "Stay healthy!"

"Thanks. Bye," I say as I stare off at the window, wondering what else I don't know about this place. The longer I'm here, the more I begin to realize just how deep the roots run.

This House has been running on its own for years without my or anyone else's knowledge. Just the elite know about its existence, and it's that fact that keeps it from falling. It's a well-oiled machine passed down from the old to the young for God only knows how long, and I am just a tiny little writing on a single paper in that giant book from his study.

Maybe that's why he was so afraid that I would run. If any word of this got out in the real world, they'd be caught, and all hell would come raining down. Eli would obviously want to avoid that at all cost, so no wonder he would take so many safety measures to keep us all contained.

And with my escape, I could've set all that information loose.

He was probably scared I would.

I frown to myself. I don't even know why I care, but somehow that little tidbit makes me smile.

Even when I thought I had no power ... I did.

And still, I let him drag me back here because I thought they held all of it.

Suddenly the door opens up again, and I'm surprised to see Dr. Audrey again. "I, uh ... I feel a bit silly, but I forgot to check for something. And I think it's important."

I frown as I sit up in bed. "What?"

She closes the door behind her and fishes something from her pocket. "Can you take this for me? I just wanna be sure, that's all. It could be the reason for your fainting."

She hands me a box, and the words inscribed on top make my eyes widen and my stomach flip. My hand immediately covers my mouth as I squeal.

"No," I mutter, and I jump from the bed, throwing the blankets off me so I can run straight into Eli's bathroom.

"Calm down!" Audrey calls out right as I lock the door. "It could be something else."

I don't respond. I don't know how to. Words escape me as panic floods my veins. Because this thing right here ... is the worry I've carried with me ever since I came to this godforsaken house.

Because for all this time spent in this luxurious cage, not once have I had my period.

I sit down on the toilet half-naked and with shaking legs, trying to keep my cool while I unpack the stick, but it's not working. Sweat pools at my back as I position it between my legs and pee a little.

"Amelia?" Audrey knocks on the door.

But all I can do is stare at the stick resting on the sink in front of me while I chew off my lip.

Slowly but surely, the line turns pink. And then another one.

Unbridled agony floods my body, and I scream out loud, sinking to the floor with the stick in my hand.

I'm pregnant.

# TWENTY-TWO

## ELI

I sit in the living room and stare at the fireplace. My fingers are splayed against each other as I lean over on my knees. The backrest of the couch hurts too much to lean against. My back feels like it's been raked open by the claws of a tiger.

*Still, it's not enough to quell the demons raging inside my head.*

"Sir?" I look up. Mary is standing in the doorway. "I knocked, but you didn't respond."

"Oh," I mutter with a frown. I guess I really was gone for a second.

"Are you okay?" she asks, stepping inside with a cup in her hands. "Here, I brought you some warm cocoa."

"Thanks, but no thanks," I respond when she places it on the table.

"Sorry, Sir. I just wanted to cheer you up."

I look up into her sweet eyes so full of joy when mine can only spew hatred. "I know. And I'm thankful. But nothing will cheer me up right now."

"Did something happen?" she tentatively asks.

I nod and grunt, hiding my face in my hands so I don't have to show her the emotions scarring me. "I tried so hard to keep her close, but the more I did, the harder I pushed her away. I wanted her so badly that I did anything for it … including betraying the very foundation of our House."

"What do you mean?" she asks.

I sigh. "I brought her in as a sinner, but I wanted her to become my wife."

"Oh," she responds.

She doesn't know what it means, but I do.

Because to be a wife to one of us is to be chained to this House for life. There are no returns, no backpedaling. You get married, you have babies, you continue the line, and the husband passes on the torch once the time has arrived.

"She hates me," I say. "I tricked her. I tricked her into it."

Mary grabs my hand and sits down beside me. "Don't worry, sir. It will be okay."

"It won't," I bark. "You don't even know what I've done."

Even through my suffering, I lash out at her, and she's still kind to me. "Sir, I don't need to know. All I know is who you are, and that is enough. I *know* you will make the right decision."

I stare at her for a moment as the realization dawns on me that she may be right.

"I'm not going to pry, but I know you, and I know you work hard for what you believe in, and I know in my heart you will do what's right."

"But what if I can't?" I reply.

She squeezes my hand. "I believe in you. And every guest that ever came here to be judged does too. They've seen what you are capable of. And I am sure that Amelia knows too, somewhere deep down."

I snort and look away. "Thanks for the pep talk."

I get up and grab the cup of cocoa, gulping it down in one go so I won't get any complaints.

Her cheerful smile proves my point. "Of course, Sir. Happy to help." She gets up from the couch and says, "If you need anything else, just call me."

"Sure," I say, but when she leaves the room again, I sink back into the couch again and bury my head between the palms of my hands. I wish I could bury my head into the sand entirely.

For nights, I haven't been able to sleep.

Questions swirl through my head.

What should I do with Amelia?

How could I ever make her love me again?

Could I live with it if she didn't?

Amelia's words are repeated over and over again in my head about how much she hates me and how she will never forgive me. I can't escape the irony of it all.

I once thought these same things about her.

And look at me now.

I'm completely overcome by my desire for her, the same desire which will never be reciprocated again. I don't need her words to know this is true. I could see it in her eyes, the pain, the hurt, the betrayal, all of it caused by me.

And now it will be my undoing.

Tears well up in my eyes, but I refuse to let them fall. Instead, I grab the book lying in front of me and chuck it in the fire, roaring out loud.

Suddenly, Soren marches inside. He glares at me, then throws a glance at the fire.

He quickly rushes to it and fishes out the book with his bare hands, patting it down so it's no longer burning.

He holds up the book, the handwritten pages still legible, albeit burnt on the edges. Soren looks at me with anger in his eyes. The same kind of look my father once used to throw me whenever I'd disappointed him "Why?" he asks.

I shrug. "What use is it?"

"Rules are rules," he says, and he gets up and brings it back to me, planting the book firmly down on the table. "Keep it."

His hand is still resting on top while he stares me down, as though he wants to tell me … this is what you chose. This is who you are. Who you were born into. Now stick with it and see it through … till the end.

I swallow as my fate begins to bear down on me.

Maybe he's right.

Maybe this is how it was supposed to end.

I look up at him. "Is it too late to right my wrongs?"

"Never," he says, in that signature low voice of his that reminds me more of a bear's growl.

I suck in a breath and nod a few times. "You know what I must do then, right?"

Soren may be silent, but he's not dumb. He's been with us for so long that I barely even remember what it was like without him. And he knows exactly what makes me tick. What keeps this house from falling apart, even when it's on the brink.

"Choose. I will help you." Always so careful with the words he picks, but every one of them is as important as the other.

But he's right. I have to choose.

No matter what, this house must continue.

The sinner must be punished.

And if I wish to see this through … I must be willing to sacrifice *everything*.

\*\*\*

# Amelia

It's the middle of the night, but I can't sleep.

I haven't seen Eli since the day I fainted and found out I was pregnant.

From the moment I was fit enough to get out of his bed, I moved straight back into my own room, determined not to speak to him again. If I'm going to be a prisoner, I might as well make his life hell too.

Which is why I haven't told him about the baby yet.

How could I when I know what's at stake? When I know damn well this is exactly what he wished for? A ball and chain to keep me a prisoner for the rest of my life.

The one thing I wanted so badly not to happen happened anyway … and now I will pay the price for it. All because I was foolish enough to spend time with him in my own shower back at home.

How could I not have seen this coming? I'm so stupid.

He tricked me, used me, led me straight down the path to my own demise, and I willingly went along with it because I thought he loved me. Because I thought I could finally forgive myself and him for all the pain he caused. Because I thought, even for a moment, that we might have a future together.

If only we had stayed there.

Right there, under that shower, time stood still, even if only for a moment, and it was the most blissful thing I'd experienced in such a long time.

For that memory to now be tainted so badly because of what he's done wounds me to my core. And worst of all ... I will never be able to forget it happened to begin with.

I stare down at my belly, my hand hovering over my skin, wishing I could speak to the baby growing inside me. That I could tell it things will be okay, even though I know they won't be. But this little white lie is the only thing that keeps me going.

I wonder if Eli knows. Maybe Dr. Audrey told him. After I screamed, I heard a door slam shut, and when I finally gathered the courage to open the bathroom door, she was already gone.

But the strangest part is that no one came to ask me anything else.

No one came to inform me of what's going to happen next. Not the doctor nor Eli, which surprises me the most. If he knows I'm pregnant ... wouldn't he come running straight to my room? Tell me to be careful, tie me up to the bed so I can't harm what's growing inside me? His entire plan was to make me his wife ... and now I'm going to have this baby.

A knock on the door pulls me from my thoughts. Mary steps in, clearing her throat. "Hey. How are you feeling?"

I shrug. Not worse, but definitely not any better.

"Good," she replies. She closes the door behind her and

quickly makes her way to the closet, fishing out clothes, shoes, literally everything that's inside, and she stuffs it all into a big bag.

I stare at her and mutter, "What are you doing?"

"Packing," she says, as she makes her way to the bathroom and swipes that clean too, stuffing it all into the bag, which she throws down near the door. "You look dressed well enough to go out."

*Out? Out as in out of this house?*

*Or out ... as in ... Eli wants to get rid of me after all?*

I frown as she grabs my arm. "Out? Where? What's going on?"

"No time to talk. We have to move. Now." She drags me out of the room and along the hallway toward the stairs. Below us, an argument ensues.

"Are you insane?! No, this goes against everything we do. You told me this would work. That you wouldn't fail!"

*It's Tobias.*

"I know, okay?! You don't have to remind me!" Eli quips.

*What are they fighting about?*

"But she changed me."

*Oh, no.*

*It's about me.*

My heart rushes as hard as we run down these stairs, and I can't help but throw a glance at the living room where Eli and Tobias are having a heated debate. For one single second, Tobias's gaze detaches from Eli's and connects with mine. Rage and confusion settle in them, and I don't quite understand what's going on. All I know is that the look he gives me makes all the hairs on the back of my neck stand.

And then there's Eli, who finally glances over his shoulder at me, and the look in his eyes is the exact opposite from Tobias, full of sorrow and misery … and regret. There are even tears in his eyes as he blinks them away, and it ruins me. Twists my heart into shapes I didn't know it could take.

His lips part. But before he or I can say anything, Mary swoops me away, into the dark of the night. The clouds above us cover the moonlight, which forces us to find our way by touching the stone. Even though it's cold outside, Mary doesn't shiver like me. She's relentless in her pursuit of a door, and when she finally finds it, she opens it wide.

"Get in," she says, her energy infectious.

I don't think asking questions is a good thing right now. Not when there's obviously haste. But I still fail to understand why. Why was Eli fighting with Tobias? And why am I being whisked away in the middle of the night?

I swallow as Mary brings me to a car and opens the door, pushing me inside the back seat. Before I can say a word, she slams the door shut and gets behind the wheel. She starts up the engine, presses a button, waits until the garage door opens, and drives off.

It only registers after a few minutes that I'm being driven away from the House.

Away from the women who are still stuck there.

Away from Eli, who was fighting over me, who told me

he still cared, despite everything I said.

Away from it all.

And something deep down inside me tells me this wasn't how it was supposed to go.

How it was planned.

And for some reason, it feels like I won't ever see this place again.

# TWENTY-THREE

## Eli

"What the hell have you done?" Tobias growls. "Sending Soren off like that just to accompany some girl?"

"You know why. April doesn't have anyone to pick her up. She wasn't sent here by her family," I reply. "And she didn't belong here either."

"I don't care!" He's never been this upset with me, and I understand. "Do you have any idea how dangerous all of this is?" Tobias barks at me, but I'm numb, even to his words. "Our whole House could be destroyed, thanks to you!"

"The sinners will not betray us. They know how powerful we are and how far our reach goes," I say, standing my ground.

Still, I can't help but stare woefully at the large wooden door, the front entrance to our house, realizing I will probably never see her again.

"Why would you do this?" Tobias asks, slamming his fist into the wall. "You *let* this happen. You were supposed to choose a woman and make her a wife, but you fell for the only one you couldn't have. For what? Was she worth it all? She got out! Again!"

I turn around and face him. "Like you wouldn't do the same thing."

We stare off for a moment, the tension like lightning striking our hearts, splitting us in half.

Men, driven by rules but fueled by wishes they know they shouldn't grant.

"I would never," Tobias replies.

"Maybe I should ask Anna, see how she feels." When I turn around, he blocks me in my path by slamming his hand into the wooden door, closing it.

"Stop."

I turn to meet his gaze. "I am not the only one who's been lying to myself."

His face darkens. "Yeah, well, I'm not the one who decided to destroy this place."

"I'm not," I reply. "They won't talk. They've been instructed not to, and they know the consequences if they do."

"Oh, and that's supposed to make this safe?" he scoffs. "They weren't done with atoning for their sins."

"I decide when they're done, and they were done. As was she," I say. "And you know what? I am too."

He frowns as I walk to the table and pick up the book that has tormented me for so long. I hold it out to him. "It's yours now."

"Wait, what?" His eyes widen. "You can't …"

"I can. And I will."

I try to hand the book to him, but he won't take it. "No, I refuse."

"Oh, c'mon. You know you've wanted my job from the very first day we started."

When I shove the book against his chest, he clutches my hand along with it.

"Eli. You know what that means. When you quit …"

I stare into his eyes and nod. "I know."

He swallows. "As your advisor, I can't let you do this." His voice is bold and unwavering. "You know why. I can't let you make the same mistake my father allowed yours to make!"

Our eyes connect again, this time not in rage but in anguish because he knows exactly what I'm about to do. What it costs for me to push everything aside. What it means for me to atone for my gravest sin.

\*\*\*

**Ten years ago**

With my hands covered in mud and blood, I waltz back into the house with my head held high. The guards step aside for me. No one dares to say a word.

Not because they have never seen blood before because they have, plenty of times.

But because I went outside with my father and came back without him.

Fearlessly, I saunter into the living room and slouch down on the couch, not giving a shit that I'm covering all the fabric in filth. I don't care who sees or who knows.

What are they going to do?

A bulky man with an equally burly beard comes barging in. Lucas, my father's advisor. The man who was supposed to have his back.

He comes to a halt in the middle of the room and stares me down. I stare back, unwavering.

"What did you do?" he growls.

"I buried him." And there isn't a single tear I will shed for him.

His stance grows firmer, as though his feet have been planted into the very wood lining the floors. "Why?"

I lean over and grab the book lying on the table right in front of me. I throw it at him, the book falling open right where my father's blood marks the page.

I point at it. "There. That right there."

He gazes down at it only briefly before looking right back at me.

It's the marriage vow he made to my mother.

He would love and cherish her until his dying breath.

"He broke his vow," I growl, glaring up at him because

he knows what this means. "You were supposed to make him keep his promise. To keep him accountable."

Lucas looks at me, his nostrils flaring.

"You knew what he did, and you never once tried to punish him," I say. "When you knew the rules by heart."

Still, he says nothing.

"Well, I did your job," I scoff.

"Are you proud?" he asks.

My eyes twitch as I narrow them. "What are you going to do? Punish me for doing *your* job?"

He steps closer and picks up the book from the floor.

"You should've protected her," I say through gritted teeth while he continues to stare at the page that has his seal on it.

He grumbles and closes the book, then plops it back onto the table. "I know I failed."

I frown. I was not expecting that.

When he turns around, I open my mouth. "What are you going to do? What about this house?"

He glances at me over his shoulder. "You're the successor. So do whatever you want. It's yours now."

My lips are still parted, but I don't know what to say as he walks away. "You're not going to stop me?"

"It's your right. This is what your father trained you to do." He sighs and pauses for a moment. "And you are right. I failed in my duties. So I will leave and repent on my own terms. Alone." He throws the keys to the basement down onto a cabinet in the corner. "I'll tell my son that it's time to take over for me. Maybe he'll do better."

***

**Present**

A long time ago, I thought no one would ever be able to surpass me, that no one could do justice as I could. Until it was my time to take over, and Tobias became my advisor. His sense of justice always managed to make me feel like I could never live up to the task. Like I wasn't meant for this role.

*He* was. And I can't help but admire him now that I've finally come to terms with that.

"That's exactly why I *must* do this," I say, making him take the book. "And you must accept this."

"You can still fix this," he says, placing a hand on my shoulder. "Bring them back. Bring *her* back."

I would've expected nothing less from him, but it's too late. I made my choice long ago.

"I can't," I respond.

"Why?" he asks, his voice full of despair.

Because he knows as well as I do how this will all end.

The answer should never be this simple, but it is. "Because I've fallen in love."

He gazes at me, his eyes filled with surprise but also something else … empathy. And for a moment, it's as though we bonded over this mutual feeling of hopelessness when it comes to our own desires.

"We must do what's right," I say with conviction. "Even if it goes against everything we've been taught."

I stand in front of him with my head held high even though I am not proud of what I've done. Of all the things I've thrown at my precious angel … of all the problems I've caused to this house …

All of this will end with me.

# TWENTY-FOUR

*Amelia*

Mary drove the car straight onto a ferry that had docked on the pier near the edge of the island, which took us across the water. She didn't stop until we reached the city where I came from.

The city where it all started.

But something about this place feels sour to the bone now. It's like it's been stripped of all the joy it once had. Or maybe that's just because I've forgotten how to love it.

She's been silent the entire way, and I don't even know where to start or what to ask. But I've been dying to know so many things, and I just pray she has the answers.

"How long will I be here for?" I ask, not even knowing for sure if I'm truly out of there.

She shrugs as she parks the car. "As long as you want. It's your life."

"But … what about the house? What about … Eli?" I can't even get his name across my lips without feeling a pang in my stomach.

"It's done," she says. "You've completed your atonement, right?"

I stare at her in disbelief. "Yes, but Eli brought me back after."

Her brows rise. "I don't know why he made the decision … but what's done is done."

I frown, clutching the bag she gave me. "I'm confused. Did you decide to just help me escape?"

"No," she says without even a hint of doubt. "You were supposed to leave."

My lips part, but I don't know how to respond as my mind goes entirely haywire.

Mary sighs. "Look, I don't know what's going on in Eli's mind. I don't know what you've done, but I know that he's changed. That's for sure."

I'm stunned she would say that. "Why? What do you mean?"

She drapes her arms over the wheel with a sigh. "When I last spoke to him, he seemed distraught at the thought of losing you. And then he lets you go. It just doesn't make sense to me."

*Eli let me go. He actually chose to let me walk?*

All this time, I thought it was Mary's choice. That she

had decided she was going to help me escape and did it in a not-so-secretive way. But now that I think about it, we were so obvious. I even looked Eli straight in the eyes as we ran.

But of course he knew. In fact, it must've been his idea for Mary to take me.

I swallow down the doubt even though I find it so hard to believe, but I am here, in the flesh, alive and in the outside world.

"I don't know what happened between you two, but I saw the pain in his eyes, and I know that whatever it was, it hurt him gravely," she says.

She looks me in the eye, making it hard to look away even though I desperately want to ignore what she just said. But it's hard, so damn hard. Because no matter how much I tried to tell myself I don't care … I do.

He's not the only one who's changed.

"Well, anyway, I don't want to derail you." She grabs a small purse and opens it up, pulling out my phone and my wallet. "These are yours."

I'm torn from my thoughts and dropped back into the real world. The world in which I'm finally free.

"Thanks," I say as she hands me back the personal items that Eli confiscated when he first took me. My hand hovers over the door handle. "So I'm … free? Completely free?"

"Whatever you wanna do, go do it," she says.

"And he's not coming back to chase me?" I ask.

She shakes her head. "I don't think so."

I pause as she smiles. "This is so strange."

She shrugs again. "Sometimes life is strange." She leans over me and opens the door for me. "Now, go. Live your life. Have fun."

I smile and give her a quick hug. "Thanks."

"You're welcome," she says.

I swiftly push the door open before she changes her mind. The smell of fresh air, the sound of people bustling about, it's all just a little too much, and I start to cry.

Home again. For the second time.

True freedom to do and go as I please.

Yet it still feels like a hollow victory.

I sigh as Mary waves at me one last time before she drives off, and I'm left with a feeling of disconnect, a feeling of not belonging. As though I've been stripped of the thing that made me … me.

I sigh and close my eyes, trying to center myself, but the noise makes it hard.

I wonder if it'll ever get easier … by myself.

I shiver at the thought.

Having to face this world alone was never my strongest point, but now? Now it feels like a monumental task, especially without him.

Eli.

I don't know why, but I can't stop thinking about him.

About how he's still in that House, chained to his own rules, while I'm here out in the free world. Did he ever think of just letting it all go? Of abandoning it all and running away with me?

I walk toward my old apartment building, but I can't shake my thoughts of him. Of what he's doing right now or whether he's thinking about me. I don't know why I care so much or why I'm even thinking about it, but I am.

He let me go.

Of all the things I expected him to do, that was not it.

He made it very clear that he intended to keep me as a prisoner, even when I vowed never to love him back. So why the sudden change?

Was it because of how I reacted to him showing me the woman who seduced Chris? Because I wanted him to let her go, despite my infernal hatred for her?

Or was it because of something else?

I step into the elevator and rub my arms, feeling cold to the bone. When the doors close and I'm shut off from the world, it feels like the silence will kill me.

I'm not used to this feeling of despair, this hopelessness, and I hate it. The only time it disappears is when I think of having his arms around me, keeping me warm.

I sigh to myself.

When did I fall?

Was it so easy that I didn't even notice?

The thought makes me want to slap myself. I'm foolish for ever having wanted a man like him. For ever letting him get close because I thought I could change him. Because I thought he would save me from myself.

But as the doors of the elevator open, I can't even bring myself to move.

Maybe his intent wasn't just to save me.

Maybe it was for me to save him.

A shiver courses up and down my spine, but I ignore it and step out into the hallway. The familiar musty smell of my building calms me. My apartment is right up ahead. My heart is pounding. Right in front of it, I pause and listen. There aren't any sounds. Maybe the landlord hasn't rented it out yet. Maybe I still have time.

Besides, it's okay to have a peek, right?

I rummage in the bag Mary gave me and find my key. She even packed it for me, and it warms my heart. "Thanks," I murmur even though she can't hear me.

I push the key into the lock and open the door. Looking around wouldn't normally make my jaw drop, but now it does. The entire place is exactly how I left it, but now it's spotless. There are new curtains, a new bed, and a whole array of potted flowers scattered around.

A wholesome warmth fills me to the brim as I walk around and touch the curtains and sit down on the bed, which is super soft and bouncy. I quite like it. But who did this? My landlord?

A pang of guilt hits me hard.

Maybe he did this because I'd vanished again, and he's already rented it to a new owner.

*Shit.*

I quickly get off and make my way back to the front door before I'm caught in the act of trespassing. But as I rush out, I squeal. My landlord stands right there in the hallway, staring at me.

"Amelia, so nice to see you," he says.

I frown, confused. "It ... is?"

*It's almost as if he was expecting me?*

"Yeah, I just wanted to thank you for paying off the rent," he says, chuckling. "And then some."

"Paying off?" I mutter. I didn't think I could furrow my brows even harder, but apparently, I can. "But I have no money. Can I stay?"

He smiles. "Of course! You can stay for as long as you like. It's yours now." He throws me another key that I barely manage to catch. "Plus some storage on the house."

"*On the house?*" I repeat.

I don't know what to say. It feels like I'm stuck in a dream.

*What's happening?*

"But I ..." I stammer. "I didn't do anything."

Why do I always have to ruin the moment with honesty? Can't I accept stuff given to me for once without trying to make things fair and truthful?

"Oh, I know," he says. "An anonymous sponsor paid off your rent plus interest and bought the place under your name."

My jaw physically drops, and I'm having a hard time breathing.

*An anonymous sponsor?*

*Paid off ... my apartment?*

"Have a great day!" my landlord says, winking.

When he turns around, I clutch the door and yell, "Wait!"

He turns and looks at me like I've lost my mind.

"Who paid it off? Do you know?"

He shakes his head and shrugs. "Beats me, but you sure are blessed with a little angel looking out for you."

*Blessed with an angel ...*

*Or maybe it was the devil trying to buy his way out of sin.*

My landlord saunters back to his own little palace while I close the door behind me and stumble backward as the world seems to spin around me.

That's when I notice the card stuck between the flowers standing on the kitchen counter. It's a handwritten note. I pick it up and read it.

*Amelia,*

*Nothing will ever make amends for the pain I have caused you.*

*But I still wanted to try to make the transition for you as easy as possible. Your apartment is yours. No questions asked. Your job at the library is waiting for you.*

*Please do not return to the strip club. You don't need their money as all your debts are paid off.*

*You've grown into such an amazing woman, so full of spirit and devotion. It commands respect.*

*You were right. You deserved better. You deserve everything and more.*

*All that I cannot ever give you.*

*I am bound to my House as you are bound to freedom. And I understand that now.*

*I know I have no right to ask anything from you, but I still wanted to beg you to consider my last wish.*

*Live a happy, content, full life.*


*With all the love I could ever possibly give in my life,*
*Eli*

# TWENTY-FIVE

## Eli

**Days later**

The halls are silent without her.

I miss her so badly that it hurts more than the fresh wounds on my back.

But I remind myself that the pain won't last long, and soon, it will all disappear.

As I kneel in front of the fireplace in my study, I sigh as drops of sweat trickle down to the floor in front of me. I am nothing. I fear nothing. Not even—

"Eli!" Mary bursts into my room. "I mean, sir. I heard your screams from all the way down in the kitchen."

I wave it off. "I'm fine."

She takes one look at the vile marks on my back and instantly covers her mouth with her hand. "Oh my …"

I get up, biting through the pain so that I can face my own sins.

"Why ..." she mutters, tears welling up in her eyes. "Why must you continue to do this?"

"You know why," I bark back.

"But she's gone. You don't have to—"

"That is exactly why I *must* do it," I interrupt.

The graveness in my voice does not go unnoticed.

"And I will not stop until ..."

She shakes her head. "But I thought that when the sinner had completed their punishment, they would be released. That's what happened, right?"

"No. I kept her like a pet, and now I must pay the price," I retort, grabbing my bottle of water to take a much-needed sip. I pour the rest over my shoulders and hiss from the sharp pain. It doesn't even take the edge off a little bit.

"You have to stop," she says, clenching her hands.

"Do not tell me what I must do, Mary," I growl.

"I ... I'm sorry, Sir." She gulps. "But I care about you."

"Don't," I retort. "Go help out Tobias. He will take over."

"Take what over?" she mutters.

"Everything."

Our eyes connect, and her pupils dilate with shock.

"What ... but you can't ..."

"I can and I will," I spit back. When the tears start to flow down her cheeks, I add, "Now go. I don't need your pity."

Tears well up in her eyes, and it pains me to see them, but I must look away. "Please, Sir. Don't do this."

"Those are the rules!" I yell.

My raised voice makes her step back. Good. I don't want her here. Not now. Not when I'm at my most vulnerable.

"You know the rules must always be obeyed," I add, my voice so raspy that it hurts, but I ignore it and grab the hot poker resting in the fire again.

"But you love her," she murmurs.

The word makes me pause for a moment. "Love doesn't exist when it's not reciprocated."

"What?" She makes a face, shaking her head. "NO. You fight for it!"

"I AM DONE FIGHTING!" I yell, maybe a little too loud.

But I don't care anymore.

What's done is done.

I have set Amelia free. And with that, I have committed the gravest of sins.

But I knew it when I first took her that this was the only logical conclusion to our passionate game.

"Now leave me. I have to prepare," I say, and I march to the door and close it before she can interrupt me again and try to change my mind because it won't ever work.

Rules are rules … and if I make others obey them … so must I.

***

# Amelia

The first few days were so surreal that they didn't even register properly. But the more time that passed, the more I became aware that I was truly free and that no one had followed me or chased after me. I was truly and utterly alone. And not only did that make me smile but it also frightened me a little.

I hadn't been alone in ages, not since before Chris, who mysteriously "vanished," according to his family. I told them he had disappeared on me after he cheated on me, and that I hadn't seen him since. The cops never questioned me, and his family stopped contacting me after a while.

I don't think they actually know I had something to do with it, which is a good thing, I guess.

I don't want a target on my back. Especially not while I'm alone.

I have no one to fall back on, and that hits me hard.

But what hits me the most out of everything that has happened is that I'm still very much pregnant. And that somehow, someway, Eli still released me.

Did he not know? Did Dr. Audrey really keep my secret?

I take a sip of my tea, trying not to think about it, but I can't stop myself. Because I sit here in this apartment solely because of Eli. He didn't just buy it from the landlord and made sure it was crisp and clean and had new furniture. No, he even paid off my student loans.

Just like that, I am debt-free.

No more dangerous strip club work.

No more nit-picking about what I can and can't buy.

And I even got my dream job at the library back.

How could I not be grateful for that?

Even Jamie was surprised to see me back. I don't blame her. After I told her I was moving to a different city, only to reappear here as if nothing ever happened, she would obviously think I was a lunatic.

But I explained that I had moved in with my new boyfriend, but that we broke up again and that's why I was back. I'm surprised she believed me, but I guess I can lie quite well. I simply said that it was all done and over with.

No more Eli.

And for some reason, that made my heart sink.

I thought I hated him. And after the stunt he pulled, I should.

But I can't help but feel grateful that he did all this for me without expecting anything in return. Out of all the things he could have, he wanted only me ... and then I was released.

Was it because I begged him to?

Or because I told him that I could never love him?

My hand that holds the teacup begins to shake. Suddenly, it becomes hard to breathe. I smash my lips together and put down the cup before I break that too.

When did it become so difficult to live with myself?

Just because I told myself I should hate him?

Should I despise him for what he did to me?

Even though, in the end, he still set me free.

It has to mean something, and I can choose to let it slide … or I can choose to care. To care about that choice. Because it matters.

It matters that he let me go.

It matters that he chose to do the right thing.

Even though he was wrong for making me go through all that pain, he tried to make it right by giving me more than enough to live on and by making sure I'd be all right.

But is it enough to forgive him?

And does it even matter when I will never see him again?

Something about that thought makes my already small heart shrivel up into dust.

Suddenly, a hurried knock sounds on my door, and I almost jump up from the couch because of the scare. More knocking ensues, so I quickly make my way to the door.

When I open it, Mary almost bursts inside.

"Amelia, hey. It's so nice to see you," she says, clutching her fingers.

"Um … yeah." It's only been a few days. I thought she'd go back to the mansion to help Eli, as that's where she works. Why would she be back here? "You wanna come in?"

"Of course. Thanks," she says, sucking in a breath before stepping inside. "I'm sorry for bursting in like that."

"It's no problem," I say, snorting. "I just hadn't expected to see you again."

She laughs. "No, me neither."

I enter the kitchen and grab a cup. "Want some hot tea?"

"Uh, sure," she mutters, so I pour her some.

She seems oddly confused, which is really unlike her, for as far as I know.

"So how are the other women?" I ask, trying to break the ice.

"I don't know. I haven't seen them."

I stop in my tracks and look at her. "What do you mean?"

She looks up at me with innocent eyes. "Well, Eli released them too."

My heart almost stops beating right then and there.

"What about Anna?" I ask.

"She's still there," Mary responds, raising her brows. "Out of her own free will."

"And the others?"

"Gone."

I grab the kitchen counter for support. "Even … the men and the woman in the basement?"

Her nod makes my lungs suddenly stop taking in

oxygen.

I have to physically lean over and force myself to breathe.

He let out all the sinners. He freed them all ... even though they hadn't atoned for their sins.

*Did he do it ... for me?*

*Because I asked him to?*

"I was as surprised as you were when he asked me to," she says.

"When?" I ask, my eyes boring into hers.

"Um ... just before I took you away from there," she answers, adding to my shock.

It takes a while to register.

Not only did he free them, he did it before he freed me. And I never even knew.

He didn't tell me or come to show off to feel good about himself. He didn't ask me if I was happy or if I would stay with him for giving me what I wanted.

He did none of that.

Because he knew it was too late.

Too late for forgiveness.

Too late for me to ever love him back, no matter the gestures of good faith.

And he did it all because of me.

When her eyes flash back and forth between me and the clock, I ask, "What's wrong?"

"Well, the thing is ... I didn't see any other option," she says, sitting down at my table but not quite relaxing. "I came here because of Eli."

"What about him?" I pour the hot water in the cup.

Maybe the fact that I found out that he did something kind and good makes me want to hear this.

"Well, you know how he has these rules he has to follow, right? Did he tell you about them?"

"No, not much anyway ... I guess the only part that I know was about me. About punishing the sinners," I reply.

"Okay, I wasn't going to tell you this myself, but I think you should know. Did he never tell you that the one who punishes is also a sinner?"

I pause and look up. "You mean like ... a sinner?"

She nods. "That's why the job is so hard. A sinner must be punished, so the punisher then also becomes the sinner, purely for hurting the sinner."

"Oh ..." I mutter, looking down at the swirling tea, wondering why she's telling me all this.

"Anyway, all the men have these things they do to punish themselves for it," she says. "But there is a specific rule that only applies to the one who governs the house. He or she must continue the bloodline."

My hand instinctively reaches for my belly, and it already starts to ache. "He knows, doesn't he?"

"Knows what?" She raises a brow.

*So she doesn't know?*

I'm totally confused now.

Why would she come here if not to tell me he's going to make me come back because he knows about the baby? She would say the words if that was true. So then why doesn't she?

"You really don't know, do you?" I say, snorting.

"No, what is it?"

I continue to rub my belly, and say, "He got me pregnant."

Her eyes widen, but not in a good way. "Oh no ... oh no, no, no ..."

"What?" My eyes widen when hers do too.

"You can't be pregnant. That means he's ... Oh God. This explains everything." She's starting to panic while I'm standing here with a cup of hot tea in my hands.

"Tell me!" I say.

I didn't mean to speak so harshly, but I care. I care too much.

She takes in a deep breath. "Well, I don't know if I'm supposed to tell you, and I don't know if Eli even realizes I remember, but he once told me that the person who governs must pick *one* woman to be his wife, and she must bear him a child. That child will continue the line. But they can't ever pick a new one. They can't ever choose differently."

*And Eli chose me, out of all the girls he could ever pick?*

*Even though I wasn't going to agree out of my own free will?*

My stomach almost does a backflip.

"And you are no longer with him since he sent you away," she adds, "which means he failed his duty."

"So what now?" She looks at me like I'm supposed to

know the answer, but I don't.

"He never told you, did he?"

I shake my head.

"The ultimate punishment for the sins *they* themselves committed ... for failing their own rules... is death."

# TWENTY-SIX

*Amelia*

My eyes widen. My knees feel weak, and my hands unsteady. The cup drops to the floor, shattering into a million tiny bits.

"When he chose to send you away, he knew he had defied the most important rule, so he—"

My lips part. "Stop."

Everything suddenly clicks into place.

His incessant need to stop himself from going too far every time he entered my room. How hard he tried to make me remember even though he knew it would make me hate him. His need to fix me, to seek me out and make me come back with him, despite knowing I desired freedom more than anything.

He did it all because he knew this was going to happen.

Because he knew he would have to face his sins eventually.

That it would mean his death.

And he begged me.

*Please.*

I still hear him in my head, pleading for me to come with him, to stay with him, to be his.

He even showed me the real truth behind his plans, the woman he had paid to ruin my world just so he could have me. He knew what it would do to me to know this truth, what kind of agony it would inflict on me, and he showed me anyway.

Because he wanted to beg me for forgiveness.

Because he needed my love … to *live*.

And I took it all away from him because I couldn't bear the thought of being locked up in that mansion like some pet waiting to serve her husband and her child.

Because I was selfish and wanted to continue my life here in this apartment as though nothing ever happened.

And it cost him *everything*, willingly.

He gave it all up because of *me*. So I could be happy.

And nothing, not even murdering my own boyfriend, has ever split me in half as much as coming to this realization.

I cannot let him die.

So I grab my coat, pack my bag, and run out the door with Mary on my tail. "Take me to him. Now."

***

# Eli

I stand on the balcony at the highest floor of this mansion. I rarely ever come here, but I'm glad today out of all days is the one I chose because the sky is so clear and the view is wonderful from all the way up here.

Normally, it's closed off, but I've made the exception and unlocked the doors specifically for today.

I, and only I, am allowed to come here. I've made that clear to everyone here. No one tried to stop me, not because they don't care, but because they know it's impossible.

I have long made up my mind.

This is how it's supposed to end.

And if you ask me, it's a pretty gentle way to go. Compared to all the pain I've inflicted on people over the years, all the ways we made them perish, this would be considered an easy way out, I suppose.

But I have endured my share of pain all these years for all the sins I committed, and now I must pay for the gravest of them all: Losing the only woman I ever cared about.

I thought I could make her love me, but it took me too long to understand.

She was right. She was right all along, and I didn't see. But I do now.

She knew exactly what it meant to love. How it aches, how it makes you bleed.

And as I have bled for her ... I will die for her.

I throw off my bathrobe and stand naked in front of the balcony, staring blissfully off into the horizon, wondering how it will feel. My skin glows with warmth, basking in the rays of sunlight swathing down from the sky above. Not even a windy breeze can stop me from stepping closer to the edge, closer to the sun.

Choosing this over any other method is freeing.

This way, I get to decide how it all ends.

I take in a deep breath and step up on the chair I put down in front of the balcony. I'm mere inches away, and my mind can't help but drift off. Instead of death, I think about her. The beauty in her smile, the sincerity in her heart, how kind she was to strangers, how forgiving she was to those who hurt her.

How easy it was to fall in love with her.

How hard it is to fall out of it.

And even if I had known this would be the outcome, that she would never love me ... I still would have made the same choice over and over again, all while knowing it would lead to my death.

Because it meant I got to love her just for that small amount of time in my life, and that was worth it all.

I stare down at the abyss in front of me. The flight will probably last an infinity, and at that moment, time will cease to exist. But there is no more way out of this. I made my choice, and now I must see it through to the end.

This is the one and final rule of this house.

My blood on that page signified my decision to make her my wife. And when I let her go, I failed to honor the most important vow. I failed willingly, knowing it would mean the end.

The punisher of sins must be punished for his own sins.

I knew the second I took her out of that library and into my home that this was coming.

This is what I deserve. This is what it all amounted to.

I committed the one sin my father refused to pay for … but I forced him to.

And now I will force myself to pay too.

I step onto the balcony, my feet dangling dangerously to the edge.

The wind blows from all sides, almost pushing me over, but I maintain balance just to enjoy my memories of this world, even if the happy ones are so few and far between. Most of them involve her, and I'm struck by how little it all mattered in the end.

I just pray I was able to make enough of a difference.

And that, by letting her go, I was able to give her something my mother never had: A chance at real love.

I sigh out loud and close my eyes. One foot rises. I hover closer, leaning over.

"NO!"

Suddenly, arms wrap around my body, pulling me back from the brink of destruction. My mind is still there, over the edge, floating down into infinity where my soul would've shattered.

And I find myself oddly split in half.

One part already over the edge.

The other ... clinging to life.

The life that keeps me here.

I smile to myself.

This has to be a figment of my imagination.

A final push of my heart and mind to turn me insane. A fitting punishment.

"Don't you dare!"

*Amelia?*

My eyes burst open. Her hands are firmly clenched around my waist, her body weighing against mine so heavy that it makes my heart bleed.

*Is this real?*

Her fingers dig into my skin as my body still teeters on edge, but hers keep me grounded on the balcony. Her warmth spills over onto me until I finally awaken to the cold wind brush past my naked skin.

Or is it ... something else?

Something wet and cold against my back.

*Tears.*

"Please ..." she whispers.

I can no longer stop myself from peering over my shoulder, from facing my biggest sin. The woman I loved until my dying breath is right here underneath me, clutching my body as though she refuses to let go.

"I need you."

The words that roll off her tongue so freely turn me inside out, and I fail to keep the tears at bay as hers start to flow. She keeps me from falling, her arms so beautifully wrapped around my body that it becomes harder and harder to breathe, and I know right then that this is not an illusion.

She's truly here, in the flesh, even though I nearly wasn't anymore.

"Amelia ..." I mutter, turning around to face her.

She buries her head against my belly, her hands still firmly wrapped around my body, refusing to let go. "Don't do this, please."

I am undone by her words.

Stripped of everything I thought I knew I needed, everything I thought I knew about myself.

Her strength is beyond my imagination. The fact that she is here right now, pleading with me not to go through with my own execution.

Why?

I lower my head at her as she cries against me. "Why did you come?"

"I can't let you do this," she says. "Stop. Please."

"You know I must—"

"NO!" she repeats, her voice stronger than ever before. "No. You don't."

"The rules are the rules," I reply stoically. "And I must pay for my sins."

"Fuck the rules!" she hisses, making me laugh. "They

exist only to punish people."

"You know why I must be punished," I say, my hand briefly caressing her hair. "I hurt people. It's my very livelihood. And I hurt *you* ... so much."

"You think you do, but you don't," she says, and she gazes up at me with those same big round eyes as before, giving me the one look that could tear a soul apart. "You hurt me, yes. But you let me go. And you let all of the sinners go too, because I asked you to, and you never even asked me to forgive you."

An inkling of a laugh comes out of my mouth. "Mary told you, didn't she?"

"Yes, but you did that on your own, despite knowing what it would cost you. You *let* me go. Because I asked. Because you knew it was the right thing to do."

"But I stole your innocence. I made you do horrible things," I say. "I am no better than my father."

"Your father killed your mother. But I live, and I was free," she says, her voice sincere, filled with emotion. "You are *not* your father."

"What I did to you was still unforgivable."

"I don't care," she says firmly.

I don't understand how she could be so resolute.

My hand slides over her cheek, desperate for a touch, even though I know she must hate me. "But you do. You hate me. Remember how you feel."

"I was wrong!" she retorts. "Please, stay with me."

*Has she changed her mind about me?*

I look down at her, clenching my teeth. Even if she has, it doesn't change what I did. "If I don't do this, the House and its rules mean nothing."

"I don't care. I am not losing you too," she says.

I'm struck in awe at her conviction.

"I'll hold you for as long as it takes." She steps onto the chair with me. "And if I have to, I'll jump down with you."

The adrenaline suddenly kicks into gear, and I grab her. "No."

"Give me one good reason," she spits back.

I look her deep in the eyes. "The baby."

Her pupils dilate, and it takes her a few seconds to respond. "You knew?"

I nod, as my eyes hover down to her belly where my son or daughter is growing. "Dr. Audrey doesn't keep secrets from me."

"And you *still* chose to set me free?" she asks, her face completely scrunched up as though she's on the verge of more tears.

I don't look away and nod. "It was your wish to be freed and not to raise a child in this home. It took me some time to realize … But you were right. My own childhood was horrible, filled with grief and the feeling of not belonging. I don't want anyone else to go through that." I swallow. "I already granted you one dark wish, and I knew I had to grant this one too. It was the best choice, and I don't regret it. Not even if it cost me my life."

The silence that follows feels like it lasts an eternity, and it hurts to see the look in her eyes, so full of melancholy but also something else ... undying sympathy. And out of nowhere, she grabs my face and plants her lips onto mine.

# TWENTY-SEVEN

*Amelia*

I kiss him harder than I ever have before.

It's not the kiss of a longing lover or a kiss of goodbye.

It's a kiss of mercy.

A kiss filled with love and devotion.

A kiss that says … I need you, and I don't want you to go.

Saliva mixes with salty tears as I kiss him, not giving a shit that we're on the edge of the world and about to fall off. If that's what it takes to keep him with me, I'll do it. I want to face whatever it is that comes our way together.

Because what does freedom really mean if you don't have the one you love to share it with?

I tried so hard to suppress my feelings for him and keep

them buried under a layer of hatred. But the second Mary told me he set the others free and was going to end it right here, right now, because that's what he was supposed to do according to the rules, I knew I had to stop lying to myself.

I had to face the one and only truth that I have never wanted a man to be mine more than I did Eli.

That is the only logical conclusion to the pain I'm feeling right now, when he is on the verge of disappearing from this world, leaving me breathless, confused, and alone.

And the sheer realization of that option made me want to cry out and call his name.

Made me jump up and run to him to hold him tight and tell him to never let me go again.

Because no amount of hatred can ever substitute the need I feel for him.

Resentment isn't the opposite of love.

You don't get so angry with random strangers.

You can only hate someone you love so deeply that it destroys you.

That you wished they had done something differently so you wouldn't ever have to hate them.

And yes, I was mad at him, completely and utterly enraged at what he had done. But all the lies and betrayal fade compared to the kindness he showed the other women. And to *me*.

Because out of all the things he could've done, he chose to set me free.

He *chose*, willingly, to relinquish me of the burden to

become his. For our child to become a part of this mess.

And with it, he chose death, knowing it was the only path he could take.

But I refuse to let him go there.

"I need you," I whisper between kisses. "Please, don't go. Don't leave me."

He presses another soft kiss to my lips, the left side quirking up into a smile. "I don't understand ... You should hate me. You should want me dead."

"No. I want you to live. I need you to stay with me," I say, wrapping my arms around his neck. "And if you really have to do this ... then I'm coming with you."

"Why would you do that?" He shakes his head.

A tear escapes my eyes as I press my lips onto his again. "Because I ... I love you."

His lips part, and he looks me in the eyes, and at that moment, everything else ceases to exist. And he smashes his lips on mine so violently that it feels like I'm being thrust right back into all the emotions I've tried so hard to keep hidden.

But it's too late now. They're out there in the open, and I refuse to shove them back down again.

Now I understand why he said he needed me ... to live.

Not because he wanted *me* to live.

But if I left ... he *couldn't* live.

And the mere realization of that hurts me to my core and makes my heart bleed.

The longer our kiss lasts, the more his feet move away

from the edge. He moves down to the chair again, to my level, our lips still firmly locked in what feels like an eternal battle of push and pull.

When he briefly takes his lips off mine, I whisper, "I'm sorry. I wish I had known sooner that this was the reason, that this was what you meant when you said you needed *me* to live." Tears well up in my eyes at the thought of losing him. "I'm sorry. I need you. I don't want you to go."

He wraps his big arms around me and presses a kiss to my head. "If you want me to stay ..."

"Yes!" I scream. "Ignore the rules. I need you. You don't have to pay for your sins."

He licks his lips. "Everybody does."

"Well, then take them out on me. I don't care!" I know I'm shouting, but I need him to listen to me for once.

His eyes are a combination of sweet love filled with misery. "You would do that for me?"

"Yes. In a heartbeat," I reply. "I would carry your sins like you carried mine."

A rich and honest smile appears on his face while he still cups mine, deepening his gaze. "I cannot let you do that ... But if this is really want you wish ..."

"This is what I want," I say. I don't need him to say anything else. "Stay here. With me."

I pull him farther down along the same chair he climbed upon. Even though he's completely naked, I still hug him tight, not wishing to let him go for fear of what might happen. Of what he might do.

"I won't let you go until you promise me you won't do it," I say, my arms still wrapped around his neck while we stand on the balcony.

"What will it take for you to believe me when I say I will grant you your darkest wish yet?" He raises a brow.

I frown. "Darkest wish?"

His thumb caresses down my cheek and across my lips. "To keep me here as an eternal slave to the suffering I caused you."

*Is he still sad about hurting me?*

*Am I the one keeping him in these chains of sin?*

Rubbing my lips together, I lean in and whisper into his ear, "I forgive you."

His breath comes out ragged, but a long-drawn-out sigh follows. And he sinks to his knees with me still in his arms. And we hug tighter than ever before.

"Thank you," he mutters, the very sound of his cracked voice breaking my heart.

My hands caress the back of his neck, as well as his shoulders, which are covered with bumps and scratchy ridges that feel awful to the touch. And as he leans forward onto my chest, I lean over his shoulder to look at what he's been hiding for so long.

Scars on top of scars, some old, some new. Painful red marks everywhere, fresh ones too, and they look like brandings. Like they were made with fire.

When I touch one of the redder ones, he hisses and arches his back.

"Did you do this?" I murmur.

He groans. "I never wanted you to see it."

I shake my head. So this is why he never let me touch his back. Why he would hide in shirts and never go fully naked in front of me.

I lower my eyes to look into his, hiding behind a curtain of hair. "Is this how you punished yourself?" I ask, trying to be as gentle as I can.

He averts his eyes and nods. "It's how we repent for the sins we commit by hurting others for theirs." He swallows. "And I've earned each one of them."

My hand reaches over to his back again. And he looks up, his eyes filled with pain. "It reminds us that we are all sinners and that we will all face the same fate."

The same fate. *Death*.

Everything that happened has all led up to this moment. And I can't help but feel in awe of the raw power this pain exudes, even if it's gnarly. Each one of these painful scars hides a story. He applied the pain to make sure that he would feel the same pain as the sinners did.

If that isn't devotion ... I don't know what is.

I touch his naked skin, which still glows red from the fresh wounds. The freshest of them all causing the most anguish. "Did you do this because of me?"

He nods, and the hurt in his eyes undoes me.

No wonder he hated being in my room with me. Every second of every punishment he applied, he gave back to himself again and again until his skin was full of scars and he had nothing left to give.

Except his life.

I lick my lips at the sight of him, wishing I could mend all of the scars and make them disappear.

He doesn't deserve to hurt for trying to make the world a better place.

He turns and grabs my hand to stop me from touching him further. "Do you hate me now? I have the scars of a monster."

A compassionate smile forms on my face. "It only makes me love you more."

His face darkens. "Don't say that. Don't—"

I press my lips to his, unable to stop myself. I cannot let him do this to himself. He needs to see that I mean it. That I'm serious about this.

"How can you say that after everything that's happened?" he murmurs between kisses.

"It isn't illegal to change your mind," I reply, wrapping my arms around his neck. "And I have. If only I'd known sooner. Maybe I could've spared you all this pain."

He cups my face with his hand, and I lean into it, desperate for more. "I needed this pain to remind me what was truly the most important thing in the world to me: You. And I would rather die than see you hurt."

"But I need you to care just as much about yourself," I say. "Please."

Our foreheads lean against each other as I gaze affectionately into his eyes. For the first time since he took me, it doesn't feel like we are forlorn lovers or captor and captive. In his arms, I feel safe and wanted, like a lover whose heart has finally been set free.

He leans in, our lips hovering close to each other, wind gushing between us. Our legs are entwined, my hands around his neck, his around my waist. And as I close my eyes, his mouth covers mine in a sweet embrace.

We kiss for what seems like all eternity, and I honestly don't want it to stop. I let him envelop me with love, just as I want to shower him in mine. I don't want to lose him. Even when I told myself I wanted nothing more … it was all a lie to protect my wounded heart.

But he stitched it back together with the wire that kept his own heart sewn together, causing it to shatter into a million little pieces. But I will fix the seam and pull him back together again.

So I kiss him back with fervor, each kiss deeper than the one before, showing my love for him. Just like our arms, our hearts are coiled together in a wicked dance, and I don't ever want it to stop.

I need him closer, deeper, endlessly, until we both perish together.

I don't want to grow old alone and unhappy.

I want him by my side forever.

And if I can't have that, then I want nothing else.

"Please," I murmur every time his lips part from mine.

"Please … what?" he whispers, his lips raw and red from kissing me.

"Please ... more."

I can feel him smile against me. And he leans in further, pushing me down to the cold stone tiles of this balcony that I've never been to before this day. He picked such a beautiful, serene place to die. No wonder he kept this place hidden from me. It would have made me cry.

But right now, all that makes me cry is how much I want him to kiss me. Because I don't know what will happen when these lips don't touch mine anymore. And I don't want to know.

All I want is to be buried beneath him, to have his eyes bore into mine, and be swept away by his love. So I open my mouth and let him claim mine with glee, happily, greedily taking in his tongue, desperate for more.

His hand rests on the tile beside me while the other cups my face, his fierce, toned body an inch away from mine. He groans against my mouth as his cock twitches against my leg, and he tears away from my lips, regret and anger settling in his eyes.

I quickly grab his face and make him look at me. "No. Don't look away."

"I can't give in to lust. No matter how badly I want you," he says, groaning as his cock hardens against my thigh. I can feel him holding back. "You deserve someone good for you."

"You *are*. You did everything I wanted you to and more. No one deserves me more than you," I reply, and I lean in for a quick peck on the lips. "Please ... believe me."

He closes his eyes and bites his lip, grunting in pain at his own desire for me. But he doesn't need to fight it.

"Please," he repeats in a low voice, groaning. "Say it again." He looks at me from underneath his dark lashes. "Say you want me. Need me. Love me."

"I need you more than I need life," I say, gently laying a hand against his cheek, caressing him with my thumb. "And I love you."

A genuine, honest smile appears on his face as he covers my hand with his. And he comes down on me once again, but this time, the kisses are far less delicate and far more fiery, filled with passion and greed. He moans into my mouth as his lips slowly go down, along my chin, down my neck, all the way to the hem of my shirt, which he pulls down along with my bra. I moan out loud when he covers my nipples and sucks on them hard.

"I love that sound … do it again," he murmurs against my skin.

I grin as he slides down my body, kissing me everywhere like he's worshipping a goddess. When he comes back up again, his hand entwines with mine, locking it above my head as he kisses me numb. His cock grinds against my pants, my back arching to meet him.

His free hand swiftly undoes the button on my pants, and his hand dives inside, straight into my underwear. The groans that emanate from his mouth set me on fire, but when his fingers find my clit, I almost explode right then and there.

His mouth momentarily unlashes from mine, a dirty grin appearing on his face. "So sensitive ... missed me?"

My nostrils flare as I make a face. "Do you want a lie or the truth?"

His tongue darts out to wet his lips right as he bites the bottom one too. "Truth."

I lean in and whisper, "I want you inside me."

His eyes almost roll into the back of his head, and the sound that emanates from his body is so twisted, so animalistic that it almost makes me come.

But he pulls his fingers away and rips down my pants instead, tearing off my panties along with it until I'm naked on the balcony tiles. My body shivers, but I can barely feel the cold as he comes down on top of me, his hand grasping my thigh as he eagerly pushes inside.

My mouth forms an o-shape as he enters me, his length so fulfilling that it makes me bite my lips too. I never thought I'd feel this again, yet here I am, getting fucked by the one man I promised I would never love.

But love has a strange way of always finding its way into people's hearts, no matter how many times they try to keep it at bay.

"I have dreamed of this moment," he murmurs against my lips as he thrusts into me. "Of loving you without repercussions."

"Then love me with everything you have."

"Everything?" he whispers into my ear. When I nod, he smiles against my earlobe. "It's all I wanted to hear."

He smacks my other hand down onto the tiles too and keeps me in place, pounding into me with everything he's got. My moans come out so loud that I'm afraid someone will hear us, but he immediately covers my mouth with his, as though he could read my mind.

My legs wrap around him as he kisses me hard and fast, leaving no moment for me to breathe, but I don't even care. All I want is for this moment to last for an eternity. Just him and me on this balcony, fucking all our problems and worries away.

Suddenly, he unlatches from my mouth. "Fuck, I'm going to come." He pulls his dick out, and I look down to see it pulse.

"What are you doing?" I ask.

"You didn't want me to—"

I wrestle my way from underneath his hands and grab his dick. "I want you. *All* of you." I swallow. "I want you to come. Inside me." It's hard to say it out loud. To admit my own desires to him.

But he accepts them with such grace and without any judgment whatsoever.

And with a smirk on his face that says "finally, she's submitted and truly mine," he's right back to claiming me, his hands immediately covering mine.

"All right, Angel."

A shiver runs up and down my spine. *Angel.* A word I used to despise now brings me joy.

"But know this was the last time I would've allowed you

to get out from underneath me," he growls.

I moan with delight when he buries his face in my neck and plants possessive kisses everywhere. When his cock plunges back inside again, I almost lose it and gasp out loud.

"Fuck …" he groans after a few more thrusts.

The way his body moves over mine pushes me over the edge, and I fall apart together with him, my orgasm coming in wave after wave as he is plunging into me. His whole body quakes as he releases his seed inside me, and I can feel his warmth filling me up to the brim.

We're both panting, and even though it cost us both so much energy, I know he's struggling. His body has already endured so much, and then to fuck me on top of it all … it amazes me.

He leans down on one elbow, his breath close to my ear. "I … love you."

Tears well up in my eyes. "I love you too."

He looks up, and even though there is pain in his eyes, there's also hope. Hope for a better future together. "You don't know how much I've longed to hear those words."

I smile up at him, but it's a bittersweet smile because I know what must follow.

He sighs as he gets up on his knees. "But I will not allow you to stay."

I lean up on my elbows, gazing at him in his full glory. The beauty that encompasses him is almost too much to behold. He's like a sculpture, so perfectly crafted yet so full of blemishes and flaws.

Is that how he saw me too when I first came here?

How he sees me now?

Suddenly, a door behind us unlocks. Someone steps inside. I don't hear it, but I see it on Eli's face.

I glance over my shoulder. Mary.

# TWENTY-EIGHT

*Amelia*

"I ... Oh my God." From the sound of her voice, she definitely saw us. "Excuse me, I didn't want to interrupt, but ..."

Eli's face turns completely possessive when he glances at me, and he calls out to her. "Bring me a blanket."

"Of course, sir," Mary mutters behind her hand, and she quickly grabs something off the couch, which she hands to him without looking. "Here."

"Thanks," he replies, and he throws it over his shoulders, then picks me up in his arms, wrapping us both inside like a burrito. My heart swells with warmth.

"Mary, could you ...?"

She hops away. "Oh, of course, Sir. I'll leave you two to

it."

"Thank you," he replies.

She tiptoes away hurriedly, but when she gets to the door, Eli opens his mouth again. "Wait."

She pauses.

"I owe you," he says.

Their eyes briefly connect, and after a while, Mary smiles and nods slowly.

He's right. Words cannot repay what she did for him. For me. For us.

She came to me when she knew the risks. It could've cost her her job.

"Thank you," I mutter at her, my cheeks glowing when she smiles back at me too.

"You're welcome," she replies, and she walks out the door with her head held high.

"You should give her a raise," I say.

He chuckles. "Already did."

I smile back. It's the first time I can look at him without feeling resentful at my own emotions, without feeling like I need to fight him off. In the frigid air, Eli's body keeps me warm. And I never realized just how much I missed being this close to him. My body was starving.

I reach for his hand, and when our fingers touch, his eyes home in on mine.

"What are we going to do now?" I ask, my heart is so heavy that it weighs down on me.

"I cannot let you stay here," he adds. He already said it

before, but I was hoping he didn't mean it. "I won't allow it. It's too toxic. You have to go."

"Come with me," I say in the spur of the moment.

His pupils dilate. "What?"

"Come home with me," I say, entwining my hand with his. "Leave this house. Stay with me instead, so we can rebuild our own life. Together."

"But I'm supposed to …"

"Are you still in charge?" I ask, frowning. "You were going to die. I know you gave it up."

He sucks in a breath, still looking at me, uncaring about the fact that we're both naked on the cold tiles. "I gave the book to Tobias. He will run this house in my place."

"So then … there's no reason for you to stay here," I say, placing my other hand on his buff chest.

He frowns. "I made a vow. It's a blood vow. And if we fail …"

"You have to die, I know," I fill in. "But you don't have to listen. Who's going to enforce those rules?" I ask. "Tobias? Is he going to make you?"

His brows only furrow more. "I … don't know."

"The book isn't sentient. It can't tell whether you are punished for your sins," I say. "I know you're trying to make it make sense, but there is none. This house only exists if the ones who govern it follow the rules. But nothing is stopping you from getting your way. From pursuing what you want." I look deep into his eyes. "Do you want me?"

He looks at me with great intent. "Yes. More than

anything. But I also want you to be free of pain."

"Then come with me so I won't be in pain," I reply. "Because it hurts to be without you."

He pulls the blanket closer. "Are you sure this is what you want?"

I smile at him. "A thousand percent."

He returns my smile. "Then I will grant you this one last wish. Even if it costs me my life, I will try to see it through to the end."

\*\*\*

# Eli

Amelia helps me put my clothes back on so I look at least presentable before we go out of the room. As I step back into the familiar hallways of my home, I feel untethered. As though the world itself has ceased to exist for just a moment. Like I shifted out of it and came back again, renewed.

When I came here, I thought I would die. That this was the end for me.

Now I'm right back where I started, back in the same house steeped in bloody history. And I can't help but wonder if I ever even belonged here. Even though I told myself so many times it was my rightful place, that I was the only heir to this house, and that I was the only one who could make it flourish … was it all worth it? Did I do it justice?

We go downstairs, and I walk into my study to quickly pick up my belongings. The picture of my mother is staring at me from my desk, and I glare right back at her wistful eyes before I sigh out loud and pack that too. I don't want this to be goodbye forever.

"Is that it?" Amelia asks.

I nod. "I don't have a lot of valuable things."

She makes a face, almost like she's impressed. "I thought you were rich after what people paid you to take care of their sinning family members."

I shrug. "I am, and trust me when I say I've put that money in a secured location out of Tobias's reach. When it comes to this house, I don't indulge in a lot of material things."

"Interesting," she muses. "So what did you plan to do with the money?"

"Use it for something good," I reply. "Like you."

Her eyes light up, and then her cheeks turn strawberry red.

"Let's go," I say, quickly leaving the room again because we don't have much time.

I pull her along with me toward the main hall. Right then, Tobias immediately comes storming out of the living room where Mary is sitting on her hands, looking completely embarrassed.

"I'm sorry," she says when she sees me. "He made me

tell him everything."

I don't blame her. Of course, she had to. I gave him the book, and the power over this house was transferred. Does he intend to use it on me?

"What the hell are you doing?" he asks me, clutching the book close to his chest. Then he looks over at Amelia, who's still behind me, and I hold up my hand to protect her from his rage. "And what is *she* doing here?"

"She saved me," I reply.

"Saved?" he scoffs. "I didn't know you wanted to be saved."

I gaze at him with no ill intent. "I don't want to fight with you, Tobias. The House is still yours. I will not be continuing my role."

He frowns, confused. "But you were supposed to ... I don't understand. What are you planning on doing then?"

"He's quitting," Amelia interjects before I can even form a response. "And he's coming with me." She steps forward now, not afraid anymore to stand by my side as my partner, my equal. Our fingers find each other and entwine, love oozing from the tips.

"Really?" He makes a face. "So that's it? This was your plan?"

"It wasn't," I reply, "but she changed my mind."

His nostrils flare, and he holds up the book like some sort of preacher. "You signed this in blood."

"I did," I reply. "I won't deny that."

"Then what do you intend to do about it?" he growls,

obviously upset because I broke another rule.

"Ignore it." I raise a brow.

His jaw slowly drops as though he never contemplated that was actually possible, and I have to admit that I didn't consider it either. Until her. "That isn't—"

"An option? Sure it is, if we make it one," I retort.

Rules aren't just there to decide our fate.

They are meant to bend according to the one who wields them.

All these years, they gave me guidance when there was no one else. But I failed to realize they were just holding me back.

My father always told me rules could never be broken.

But they were *made* to *be* broken.

And I refuse to let my father and his brainwashing chain me up any longer.

Tobias shakes his head along with the book. "You disgrace the rules. I can't let you do that. You cannot ruin everything we've built for so long."

"We didn't build this house. We kept it going," I reply. "I'm not ruining anything by simply leaving. You have taken over now, and I trust you to make the right decisions for this House." I pat him on the shoulder a few times, but he still looks angry. "Rule it as you see fit."

"So what? You think I can just forget that you made this?" He opens the page right to where I put my fingerprint in blood.

I take in a deep breath.

"What … is that?" Amelia asks.

"Eli made a vow." He glares at her now. "You are to become his wife and have his child, or he dies. Those are the rules." He throws me another damning look. Is he truly intent on making me see this through? "And you made your choice."

"No." Amelia quickly jumps in front of me. "I did. I made a choice to run."

"I *know* he let you go," Tobias says, throwing daggers with his eyes.

"Out of love," she replies steadfastly. "And I still intend to have his baby and marry him. Doesn't that count?"

My eyes widen, and I grab Amelia's shoulders and make her turn to look at me. "You would do that for me?"

She nods with a smile on her face. "If it means you get to live …" She places her hand on top of mine, and I am utterly moved by the love she exudes. And I want nothing more than to swoop her up in my arms and run off.

"You would do that for him out of your own free will?" Tobias asks, his stance growing rigid.

Amelia nods.

"What changed?" he asks.

She smiles at him. "He chose to do the right thing."

His face tightens and softens all within a second. As though he's astonished this can even happen and that it would influence her decisions too.

He licks his lips and lets out a breath. "What about the House then?"

"We will leave it to you," I say. "It's what you wanted, isn't it?"

"It doesn't matter where we go or where I have the baby, right?" Amelia asks, throwing a look at Tobias. "Or is that in your little rule book too?"

I love the little bit of added sass.

"There is no rule for that, no," Tobias sneers. "There should be, though."

I understand how he feels. I've been guided by these rules for so long that it's hard to let them go. But I must. For her.

He snaps the book shut. "I guess it's settled then. So what now?"

"Instead of dying, I continue to live," I reply. "That's it."

"Okay …" He rubs the bridge of his nose with his index finger and thumb. "I should've known this would happen, considering your history."

"At least my history brought me some valuable insight," I rebuke.

I know he's talking about my father, but it doesn't hurt me any longer. Nothing he says can touch me as long as I have Amelia's love.

Tobias narrows his eyes at me. "Do whatever makes you happy." He turns around and walks back to the living room. But right before he goes inside, he glances at us over his shoulder. "But don't ever come back because this rule changes *now*."

I nod, and he nods back. A hint of a smile perks up the side of his lip.

It's not just a threat.

It's a promise.

A promise to make my life miserable if I ever choose to leave her.

Not because he hates me or because he's jealous.

But because he wants me to succeed. Because he wants us to make it out alive and live out our days with love and happiness ... because, after everything we've done and been through, that is what we deserve.

And I plan to start being grateful for that right now, so I wrap my arm around Amelia's shoulder and pull her with me toward the door. "Let's go home."

"Home?" she murmurs, gazing up at me with those same doe-like eyes that once captivated me enough to make me want to bring her in.

But now, I want nothing more than to protect this little angel of mine. "Your home. Or our home ... depending on what you want. I can always get a new place to stay."

She raises her brows at me in a cheeky way. "Mi casa es su casa."

# TWENTY-NINE

*Amelia*

When we finally get back to my apartment, I throw everything I brought with me back onto the kitchen counter and breathe a sigh of relief. "We made it."

Eli stands there with a small bag in his hand, a little unsure of how to carry himself. I don't think he ever thought he'd be back here.

I grab his hand and lead him around. "I know you've been here before … but I thought I'd formally introduce you to the apartment." I show him the bedroom and the kitchen area along with the bathroom even though he's seen it all before.

"I know," he says eventually as we stand in the doorway to the bathroom. "Why are you showing me all of this?"

I shrug and smile while looking up at him. "Because I want it to be different. I want a fresh start."

His eyes flicker with amusement. "So you want me to stay?"

"Yeah, that's what I said." Why would he ask again? "What other option is there?"

"But Tobias isn't watching us. There are no cameras here," he says.

"So?" I put my hands against my side.

"He won't follow me here, nor will he know what we do. It will be as though we never existed to him," he says.

"What's your point?" I ask, frowning at him.

He puts a hand on my waist and pulls me closer. "I can get my own place if you need the privacy."

I laugh, and it's the most genuine laugh I've had in a while. "Oh my God …"

"Why are you laughing? I'm serious."

I playfully slap his chest. "I am not asking you to do that. Just stay here. With me."

"I don't want you to do this out of pity," he says.

"I'm not." My hand slowly moves down toward the baby growing in my belly. "Besides, this baby is going to need his or her daddy to be there."

His eyes begin to glow with pride, and it fills me with joy. "You want to keep it? I thought you only said that so we could get out of Tobias's clutches."

I suck in a breath. "I've been thinking about it for a long time, but I can't get it across my heart not to."

His hand instinctively reaches for my belly, and I let him touch me.

"This baby was conceived right here in this bathroom," he mutters.

I nod, tears welling up in my eyes. "Out of love."

When I look up into his eyes, they are so full of affection that it tugs at my heartstrings. "Are you sure? I don't want you to regret—"

Before he can say another word, I cover his mouth with mine, sealing the deal. When I inch back for a second, a mischievous grin spreads on his face.

"You can't take that back," he murmurs against my lips.

"I don't want to," I reply, smiling right back at him.

"I don't think you realize what you signed up for."

He smashes his lips back onto mine, his kiss far more aggressive as his hand palms my back, pulling me closer against him. I don't fight it at all. In fact, I want nothing more than to wrap my arms around his neck and fall into his sweet embrace. I want him to destroy me and heal me in a single kiss. And I don't want this to ever stop.

"I tried so hard to get over you, but you've made it impossible, little Angel," he whispers. "And now you'll face the full brunt of my love. Are you ready for that?"

I gulp and nod, my pussy already getting wet just from the thought of all the deliciously dirty things he's thinking about, all the things he could do to me, all of it right within our grasp.

"No more punishing for sins," I mutter. "And no more

lies."

"Not even the dirty ones?" he groans, pressing another sultry kiss to my lips that awaken all my senses.

"Hmm, maybe ... if they lead to good things," I reply.

"Good things," he repeats. "Like this?" He whisks me up into his arms and shoves me against the wall.

"This isn't a punishment," I say, giggling as he plants kisses all over my neckline.

"Oh, but it will be if you do something I don't like," he muses. "Like hiding from me or not doing something that makes you happy."

"Oh, are you now?" I raise a brow. "And what's the punishment for that then?"

A filthy smirk appears on his face. "Pain."

And he pushes down my shirt and twists my nipples, making me moan.

Oh ... *that* kind of pain.

"I can live with that kind of pain. I definitely can," I murmur, grinning.

"Good. Because I don't intend to stop." He leans in and whispers into my ear. "Ever."

\*\*\*

When I finally go back to work again, Jamie's eyes widen when she spots me.

"Amelia?" she mutters as if she can't believe I'm actually here.

But before she can say another word, I put down a giant bouquet on her desk.

A broad smile forms on her face. "Wow, these are gorgeous."

"They're for you," I say, a blush on my cheeks from her reaction. "As a thank-you for all the help you gave, and an apology of sorts for my behavior."

"Aw, you shouldn't have," she muses. "But thank you so much. I did wonder where you were all this time after you hurriedly left with that guy. I thought you weren't coming back for sure this time."

I blush. "I wasn't, actually, but things change." I rub my lips together. "And I'm coming back to work here."

Her jaw drops. "Huh? But how? I don't understand."

"My boyfriend really wanted me to have this job back, so he made her a better offer somewhere else."

Her brows rise. "Your *boyfriend*?"

Her reaction makes me blush even harder. It feels so weird calling him my boyfriend, but it's even weirder hearing it from someone else's mouth. I don't think I'll ever get used to it.

"Eli. He's the one who took me from my apartment."

"Oh, that guy." She makes a face. "And you two are dating now?"

I nod, rubbing my lips together. "He saved me."

"Saved you?" She frowns.

I chuckle. "It's complicated." And I readjust my clothing as it feels awkward to talk about all of this.

"Hey, I don't judge. I just wanna know … Is he treating you right?"

I smile. "Yeah. Better than Chris, definitely."

"Good." She lets out a big sigh.

"Are you upset with me?" I don't want to be a bother, but I want to know if we're on good terms. "I just want things to be okay between us."

She shakes her head. "No, it's fine. I mean, you were always a great coworker, and I did miss you."

I smile. "I missed you too. And being here is my favorite thing in the world."

We both smile, and I look down at my own feet as I don't know what to say to her. I've lied so many times, but I can't possibly tell her the truth either.

"I … I'm sorry for leaving you so suddenly without letting you know anything," I say.

"No, no, you don't have to apologize," she responds.

"But I do," I say. "It was no way to behave. I had some personal issues." I tuck my hair behind my ear.

"Oh … Well, as long as you're happy and safe. That's all that matters."

"I am," I say, the smile on my face growing broader. "And I just want things to be normal again."

"That's good to hear," Jamie says. "And you know what? Same, girl. Same." And she winks.

I giggle to myself while Jamie grabs a stack of books, plopping them down onto the table right in front of me. "Here. You can start right away."

I throw down my stuff and place it under the counter, then grab the stack with a happy grin. "Yes, ma'am."

***

# ELI

When I find her again, I sit down on one of the chairs near a round table in the back, closest to the bookshelves she's working on. She hasn't noticed me yet, but that doesn't stop me from staring anyway.

I enjoy looking at her from afar while she's busy rearranging the books as though she wrote them herself. My eyes follow her every move. Her fingers as they slide down the spine of a book. Her eyes as they peek at the words inscribed while her body leans into the shelf. It's like a dance between her and the books, and it reminds me of the way she always leans into me when I wrap my arms around her, and the way she always looks into my eyes hungry for my kisses, my touch … and my cock.

I bite my lip at the thought.

I can't help it.

Whenever she's gone, all I can think about is ravaging her.

I quite like this new job of mine. Description: Making my angel happy.

Watching her from the shadows at a safe distance never

gets boring. Especially not when she finally notices me.

A smirk forms on my face as my index finger rubs along my lip, her eyes tracing greedily along. My tongue darts out to wet my finger ... and then I go in for the kill.

She giggles and runs off, ducking between two different bookcases. But she cannot hide from me. I know every one of these bookcases like the back of my hand, and I know exactly where she's going.

The farthest bookcase in the back of the building, the musician section. The place no one ever goes to look.

But I'm not here to read books, and she knows.

I'm her silent stalker, and the predator has cornered his prey.

A filthy grin spreads on my lips as I clutch both bookcases and block the exit. With her back against the wall, she's trapped between me and the books she loves so dearly. But she loves one thing in this world more ... me.

I prowl closer, and her chest begins to rise faster and faster as her breaths become ragged. "Eli, what are you doing here?" she murmurs.

My brow rises. "You know why I'm here."

Her lips part, and her body, wrapped in jeans and a soft, woolen top, quivers. Her clothes barely cover her petite body, yet I want nothing more than to rip it all to shreds.

I step closer and closer until I'm towering over her. And my hand slams down against the wall behind her. With one hand on her waist, I lean in and whisper into her ear, "Tell me ... what's your darkest wish?"

A sweet, almost sinful smile spreads across her lips. "Punish me," she whispers.

I groan and press my lips against her neck, right below her ear. "Good, because I intend to."

And I whisk her up into my arms and shove her against the bookcase, kissing her until she's breathless while her fingers rip away my shirt. And I smile against her lips as she wraps her legs around my waist, eager to submit to me. I look up into her beautiful eyes laced with the same lust that courses through my veins whenever I lay my eyes on her. It doesn't matter where or when. She will always be mine. "Let's be sinners … together."

# EPILOGUE

*Amelia*

**Eight months later**

"Push! Push!" the nurse yells at me, but I can barely hear her through my own screams.

The pain is beyond belief, and I'm not sure I can hold on. But I must. I have no choice but to push on, literally. And I do, with all the strength I have left.

"You can do this, Amelia," Eli says, clutching my hand even though I'm squeezing his to death. "I know you can."

"It hurts!" I shriek.

But when I look into Eli's eyes, all I see is the same pain he's been through. The burn marks on his back must've hurt just as much. And if he could bear it, then so can I.

So I close my eyes and push on and on until my very last breath.

"Look up!" the nurse says, and when I do, there's a little head. "It's a girl."

Tears well up in my eyes as the pain and adrenaline all come rushing out of me. And I cry as the nurse hands me my baby. When her little lips part and a cry comes out, my heart swells with a love I never knew existed.

Eli presses a kiss to my forehead. "I'm so proud of you."

"She's ours …" I murmur.

"But you did all the work," he says.

"We have to give her a better life. Better than we had," I say, looking up at him, and he nods in agreement.

All the suffering I've been through vanishes from my heart when I look at her. This little girl … she was worth it all.

"I promise you now, little girl …" I murmur, kissing her on the forehead. "Your parents will love you. No matter who you are or what you do. And we will always be here for you. Always."

***

# ELI

"Right, Eli?" Amelia asks as she looks up at me from

her bed, her hair in shambles, her eyes thick, the bedding bloody and sticky from the messy birth. But none of that matters. All the pain and suffering fades when I see that wondrous little bundle of joy in her arms.

And when Amelia holds her out to me, I gently take her into my arms, cradling that beautiful girl while staring into her eyes. She has the eyes of her mother. Eyes that make my heart jump. Eyes that split my soul in half.

"She's beautiful," I whisper. "You hear that? You're the most precious thing alive."

"What should we name her?" Amelia asks.

I look down at the pretty girl in my arms, whose whole life is ahead of her. It won't be an easy life, and it will definitely be full of struggle, but I know in my heart she will do good. She is, after all, the spitting image of her mother.

"You decide," I mutter as I look up at Amelia.

"Really?"

I nod. She seems surprised I'm willing to let her decide. I don't easily hand away control, especially not when it comes to us, our lives, and our relationship. But certain things require an exception, and one of those times is now.

"Isabella," she says.

"Isabella." I look down at the sweet little cheeks that I can't wait to cuddle. "Perfect name for a perfect little girl."

"She doesn't have to be perfect," Amelia says.

I look up at her, softly swaying Isabella to soothe her.

"No ... but she is, just by existing," I reply, which makes her smile.

But then the smile dissipates within seconds. "Will she be safe?"

I frown. "What do you mean?"

"Safe from ... the House." She gulps, eyeing Isabella as though she will steal her out of my arms and run away with her if she has to, even though she's still bloody and recovering from the birth. I guess this is what they mean when they talk about a mother's love. The fierceness of it catches me off guard. Maybe because I never experienced it with my own mother.

"I won't let you take her there," she says.

"You don't have to fear that," I say, and I give Isabella back to Amelia. "She will always be yours."

"What about Tobias? Will he come for her?"

I sit down beside her bed and grab her hand. I can't believe she would ask this now even though she's asked it before, during the pregnancy. I guess, now that the baby is actually here, it's brought her a sense of urgency.

"No. The House remains his, no matter if she exists or not. She cannot ever take over since I relinquished control. His legacy isn't threatened by her, if that's what you fear," I reply.

She nods a few times. "Okay, good. Because I'd rather die than have that happen."

I lower my eyes and look at her from underneath my lashes. "As will I." I cup Amelia's face. "There is no one in this world I love more than you ... and her." I peek down at Isabella. "And I will do everything that's in my power to protect you."

"Promise me you won't ever make us go back. And promise me you won't either," she asks. "I don't want it to be a part of our lives anymore. No more punishing sinners."

I rest my forehead against hers. "You have my word."

"And you'll keep your word?"

I nod. "If you want, I will make a vow, right here, right now." I get off the bed and grab her diary, which she's been keeping ever since we came back. I flip to the page in the back and grab a knife from the kitchenette in the corner of this room. I don't hesitate to cut into my thumb, blood oozing from the skin. Amelia merely stares at me as I press my thumb down onto the page to seal the deal.

"There. This is my vow to you. I will never, ever, let anyone take you or Isabella back to that house, not even me."

She breathes a sigh of relief but then sits up straight again. "But you broke that other vow too. How do I know you won't break this one?"

"I didn't," I say with a resolute voice, and I approach her while fumbling in my pocket. "And I won't."

"But you didn't marry—"

Her lips stop moving as her eyes land on the very thing I've just pulled out of my coat. The little box I've been hiding for months contains a giant ring. I couldn't find the right time to propose to her, so I waited, and waited, and waited ... until now. Until I saw my child's face and realized I must do everything in my power to make her mother happy.

Because that is what any child deserves.

And it is what she deserves too …

*Love.*

My love, which I'm more than willing to give.

So I go down on one knee right in front of this hospital bed and say, "Marry me."

Her jaw drops, and for a second, I'm wondering if she'll reject me. But then her eyes fill with tears, and she begins to nod rapidly. "Yes. Yes!"

I grab her hand and slide the ring onto her finger, finally committing to the one vow I made so long ago.

Without waiting for another second, I press my lips onto hers with full force, not giving a shit that some of the staff pacing by the hospital room gawk at us and giggle under their hands.

I want nothing more than to love her for the rest of my life. Because that is what she deserves.

So I whisper against her lips, "I told you I don't break vows."

# THANK YOU FOR READING!

Thank you so much for reading Dark Lies. You can stay up to date of all my new books via my website: www.clarissawild.com.

I'd love to talk to you! You can find me on Facebook: www.facebook.com/ClarissaWildAuthor, make sure to click LIKE.

You can also join the Fan Club: www.facebook.com/groups/FanClubClarissaWild and talk with other readers!

*Enjoyed this book? You could really help out by leaving a review on Amazon and Goodreads. Thank you!*

# ALSO BY CLARISSA WILD

### Dark Romance
The Debt Duet
His Duet
Savage Men Series
Delirious Series
Indecent Games Series
The Company Series
FATHER

### New Adult Romance
Cruel Boy & Rowdy Boy
Ruin
Fierce Series
Blissful Series

### Erotic Romance
Hotel O
Unprofessional Bad Boys Series
The Billionaire's Bet Series
Enflamed Series

Visit Clarissa Wild's website for current titles.
www.clarissawild.com

# ABOUT THE AUTHOR

Clarissa Wild is a New York Times & USA Today Bestselling author with ASD (Asperger's Syndrome), who was born and raised in the Netherlands. She loves to write Dark Romance and Contemporary Romance novels featuring dangerous men and feisty women. Her other loves include her hilarious husband, her cutie pie son, her two crazy but cute dogs, and her ninja cat that sometimes thinks he's a dog too. In her free time, she enjoys watching all sorts of movies, playing video games, and cooking up some delicious meals.

Want to be informed of new releases and special offers? Sign up for Clarissa Wild's newsletter on her website www.clarissawild.com.

Visit Clarissa Wild on Amazon for current titles.